SWEET BRIAR WITCH

BETTINA M. JOHNSON

Aqua Raven Publishing

Sweet Briar Witch

Copyright © 2021 by Bettina M. Johnson

ISBN: 979-8-9850697-0-9 (paperback)

Cover art by Stunning Book Covers

They say if you focus on the negative, your life becomes a reflection of what you are thinking. They also say negative thinking can become a habit, which over time can become an obsession. I've also heard them say one small positive thought each morning can change your entire day. I don't know who "they" are, but right now, I have a broken coffee maker, my fiancé, Lorcan, barked at me a little at his mechanic shop yesterday when I mentioned his lack of customers, my cat, Wicked, is missing, and I have an overabundance of negative thought surrounding me.

It mostly might have to do with the fact that I slammed my favorite coffee mug down, cracking it, upon discovering my heretofore working coffee maker wouldn't turn on.

I checked the cord. I checked the wall plug. I even flicked the breaker a few times. Nothing. Nada. Zip.

It wasn't like Sweet Briar, Georgia—my hometown—had a bevy of Dunkin Donuts on every corner that I could run to and satisfy my admitted coffee addiction. And I didn't feel like subjecting myself to my usual java spots—Joe's Diner or my Uncle Stephen's Enchanté Café—this fine Saturday morning. I'd been lying low on an antisocial bent ever since I'd discovered my town hated me.

"Did you try pushing the button?"

Pandora, my crossroads demon friend, was repeatedly pushing the start button on the coffee maker over and over again, and the sound of it clicking on then off was driving me batty.

"Yes. Of course, I did," I said through gritted teeth.

"I don't understand."

"What don't you understand, Dorie? The idea of me being capable of turning on a button to start coffee or that I did and the machine didn't turn on as usual?"

"Someone's a grumpy pants."

That from my resident ghost, Edith Plank. Edith had been AWOL since before Christmas and never gave me any reason for her absence, but now she was back and the snark was flying, as usual.

Yes...I have a demon and a ghost cohabitating with me. I used to hope it a temporary thing...but they've been here for months now, and quite frankly, I just don't care anymore.

Click, click, click, click, click.

"Dorie, stop it!"

Click.

"I mean it, Dorie. It's broken! And I'm not a grumpy pants!"

Click.

My jaw was beginning to ache, and my brow was so wrinkled I probably resembled a Shar Pei dog. That I could smell my freshly ground coffee was not helping the situation, and Dorie being Dorie took it over the top—my ability to stay rational, shot.

"Who's a grumpy pants?"

Great. If my morning wasn't already a total disaster, the

voice that just entered my kitchen made it one hundred times worse.

"Adriana," Edith giggled her hello.

"Spooky. Good morning. I assume you mean my darling great-granddaughter who is grimacing and pretending she hadn't noticed me walking in just now?"

Adriana Dolce, granny extraordinaire and evilest dark witch in all the southeast, if not the world—her estimation, mind you—came waltzing into the kitchen and scrambled onto the stool at the counter. She proceeded to take in Dorie trying to turn on my coffee machine and came across as a tiny black bat...all dark cape and swinging pointy-toed boots.

"So, what's up?"

"Lily is upset because Pandora keeps turning her coffee machine on and off."

"I'm not turning it on and off. It's not turning on at all. It just makes this clicking sound that's making Lily cranky," sniffed Pandora.

"Grrrr," I grumbled.

"See?" Pandora smirked in my direction, and I bared my teeth at her. That I'd been recently turned into a vampire should have given her pause, but no one seemed to care one way or the other...and quite frankly, that rankled. I'm a badass.

No really! I am!

I can't help it if my entire family and most of my friends are themselves a bunch of paranormal freaks!

But this does take me back to why I'm grumpy—OK, fine, I am—and hiding, convinced my town hates me. You see, because I am a double dark witch—my mom is one and so is my dad, and it only means we can harness some truly awful magic but choose not to because, well, we are *nice people*. I have recently found out the Witch Council has denied my marriage banns and requested I cease and desist from anything and everything witch. You can imagine how well that has gone over with me. Little did they know, Lorcan and I managed to sneak our names in the banns book and sealed the date we intended to marry magically. We'd deal with that when our trickery came to light... but right now I hated the world.

OK, fine. I was way more concerned about Lorcan snapping at me than I was letting on. And my missing cat had me beyond worried. Not to mention the feeling that I was constantly under the microscope as of late.

While the holidays had been sweet—pun intended—life since has become ridiculous with friends and neighbors, and even a few relatives, questioning my every move and scrutinizing my spellcasting abilities.

Compound my dark witch heritage with the other stuff mixed in—vampire from taking life-saving blood from one, demon blood from Pandora, and siren blood because in some weird way, I've yet to connect, I have now been branded a Heinz 57 witch of ill repute. Everyone is concerned about whether or not I'm doing things I've been banned from doing ever since it became common knowledge about my mixed blood...and our Witch Council suggested I refrain from doing anything arcane. Even after saving this town from evil—the ingrates.

I'd even broached the subject again when I was with Lorcan yesterday, asking him if he'd regretted tying himself up with someone made up of so many different Breed. He'd assured me that we'd deal with anything that might arise from our children when and if it did. "We could always name one Heinz and the other Ketchup which would settle it." Not. Then he'd assured me our kids would be lucky having such a tenacious and powerful witch for a mother considering I'd wiped the town clean of evil.

OK, fine...so one baddie is still on the run. Her name is

Rowan Nightingale, and she's a teenaged freak of epic proportions. And I may have some topsy-turvy magic that backfires when I least expect it. But I can do amazing dark magic despite this—I just suck at the basics. You know, light a candle instead of burning down the town, snap my fingers and poof! Coffee.

"Hey, why don't I just snap my fingers and..."

"Lily! No... don't..."

BOOM!

❦

"I don't think the Jorgensons even care anymore. They didn't come out to see what happened." Pandora kept peeking through my kitchen blinds toward my neighbor's yard while tiny flakes of soot and ash rained down around us like some kind of reverse snowfall. The entire kitchen looked like a nuclear fallout, so the sooty flakes seemed to belong in a strange way.

"I don't think the Jorgensons live next door any longer," whispered my cousin Andrea in awe as she glanced around my blackened kitchen. "Would you?"

Andrea had been away taking business courses at the community college in Gainesville and had barely had much time to hang with me as of late. She had a few more months to go, then would be back riding shotgun to my adventures—or so I hoped. It looked like Uncle Stephen was backing away from the café and letting Steve Junior and Andrea take over while he and my Aunt Chiara enjoyed some together time.

Right now, Andrea was standing wide-eyed in my kitchen watching the ash and soot float down like blackened snow.

"We felt the house shudder and knew...I mean, guessed... oh dear." This from my future (or not!) mother-in-law, Eileen

Reid, who was watching her husband, Henry, examine the wreckage that was my kitchen.

"How did you...?" Henry rubbed his chin and shook his head in wonder.

"She twirled when she should have swirled. It was fantastically horrific," grinned Adriana, then made her fingers turn into a gun and shot me.

"Bam! The entire kitchen went up."

I threw the dish towel I had been using at my great-grandmother's face and crossed my arms. This just caused her to cackle anew, and I flexed my fingers controlling my urge to toss one more spell—in her direction.

"I can fix it. Just give me a few hours and it will be better than new," I argued.

"Fix it? Lily, my dear, your Uncle Owen just got off the phone with me, and if you so much as wish a spell, the Witch Council is throwing you in the shiny new prison they just finished erecting...and tossing the key into an abyss somewhere. You know they've forbidden you from doing any magic until the Meeting of Elders next week!"

"Yet I did. And I don't care. They can't do that! The Order of Origin said I'm to be given special treatment because of..."

"The Order of Origin has since reneged on that decree...you are not to perform any kind of magic until your hearing."

What? When did that happen? How could these things be decided without my being made aware of them except through secondhand information? And now I'd have to answer for my "crimes" and face yet another vote on my fate in a few days.

"But that's not fair!"

"It is what it is...and you need to abide by..."

"Nothing! I need to abide by nothing. I saved the town! I

saved my father! I got rid of Lucretia, finally, and Donna...Deanna...I mean, I'm a flipping hero!"

"She is, you know," Edith said in my defense.

I was too. I tricked that evil Deanna and managed to save my father. I kept the renegade witch clan from out west from bothering us once their leader was eradicated. They'd dissolved into nothing and ran off to hide back to wherever they came from. My mother and father were together again and had a chance at a happy life...all because of me!

"Liliana! You have magic going haywire and none of us knows why. We can't risk this family's reputation just because you feel slighted. Now, if we can only..."

"Fine! I'm leaving then." I slammed my hand down on the sooty table, making the coffee mugs bounce and Adriana frown, mouth open, words left unspoken. I would show them all. I'd just pack my stuff and move back to New York State...find a wee cabin in the woods and go live the life of a hermit.

I felt two strong arms encircle me and someone's chin rest on my shoulder. I didn't have to turn around to know it was Lorcan, trying to calm me down by shooting some of his empath juice into me. I won't say it didn't work—a little.

"You can't leave," he murmured in my ear. His soft, soothing voice sent thrilling little shivers down my spine, and I took in a large breath and let it out slowly in an attempt to calm myself.

"Why not?"

"Because my heart would break and I'd worry about where you'd gotten yourself off to, and Mister Walter's old Chrysler Imperial will never get repaired then."

"Heaven forbid."

Lorcan fixed cars when he wasn't going around town being the calm, witchy empath spreading strength and peace wherever he went. He'd already apologized yesterday after grumping at me, admitted work had been slow as of late, then went on to explain the auto business could be fickle and not to worry. He didn't want it getting out that his business had been slow since just before the holidays, and I promised I wouldn't say a word to anyone. Then we made up by spending a few moments snuggled up and kissing—always a surefire way of calming me down.

"I'm here. I can help fix this mess or just hold you. Whatever you need, baby."

"I don't need a knight in shining armor on a white horse, Lorcan."

"Who said anything about a knight? I'm a multi-trick pony. I come in, assess the situation, and put out all the fires without batting an eye. I'm a beacon of stability in a sea of turmoil."

The irony wasn't lost on me—Lorcan, the rock steady one and me, utter chaos. One can only wonder what our children will turn out to be—if we can ever make it down the aisle, that is. Mister Walter's car had been giving him fits for the better part of two weeks. Just the fact that he came running when he heard my deplorable news showed how much the big lug loves me, and I smiled. But it was a bittersweet moment.

If the Witch Council and our enemies pushing to have me branded a renegade witch get their way, Lorcan and I will never marry, have children, and grow old together. The thought made me despondent, and I felt my bottom lip quiver. Lorcan took one look at the transformation on my face and pulled me in for a great big hug.

"I've got this mess. Why don't the rest of you go settle into the den and leave me at it in here. Have some coffee." Henry, my future father-in-law, gave me a kind smile and continued to survey the mess. He is a handyman witch and could restore order when destruction—me—made things explode. I recently discovered this and, due to my lack of being raised knowing all things witch, queried as to why we don't employ our magic instead of using the mundane. Trust me, my bank account would be happier had I not spent a ton of money on home renovations. It was explained to me, however, that magic comes with a price. Even the tiniest bit of magic exacts something on the one who casts it.

"Henry. No. Please. Something of this magnitude would mean you have a high price to pay. I can't let you do this for me." I reached my hand out to Henry, and he gave it a squeeze.

"Don't you worry none, sweetheart. I have some reserve spells that won't take much, and I can't think of anyone I'd rather use them for. I will have this cleaned up in a jiffy! So go have that coffee."

"Can't. The machine is broke and..."

And I smelled fresh coffee brewing. Looking in incredulity at the coffee maker which was now chugging away, filling up the pot, I felt my lower jaw unhinge.

"How?"

"Well, looky there. Lily might have taken out her kitchen, but she managed to fix the coffee maker!" Adriana cackled, then slid off the stool and flapped her way into my den.

Why can't I ever have a nice, quiet weekend?

2

"Now, what is this I'm hearing about Wicked? What do you mean she is missing?" Adriana sat in the chair closest to the fire. January in Georgia could be cold, mild, or insane, and so far we've experienced warmer than usual temperatures. One day we'd be in the mid-seventies with nights in the forties. The next, our high temperature would barely reach fifty degrees and we'd plummet to the twenties at night only to have it ricochet up to warmer readings the next day. Schiz-ophrenic weather at its best was Georgia this winter.

"She's gone. She was here Wednesday morning, but we haven't seen her since."

It was now Saturday, and Wicked had never been gone from home this long.

"Did you say something to upset her?"

"No, she was fine. Hey! What do you mean 'did you say something to upset her?' She's a cat!"

"See? Right there. Your attitude, young lady. You probably said something you shouldn't, and now Wicked is out there all alone and frightened. Upset because you are mean," said Adriana.

Is she kidding? So much for sympathy. Adriana liked playing devil's advocate and decided poking the bear—one who still didn't have enough coffee running through her system to be civil—would be a good idea. Hint...it's not.

"Are you out of your mind? Mean? Me? And Wicked frightened? Are we speaking about the same cat?"

"Yes you. Mean. Big meanie."

"I am not mean!"

"Yes, you are!"

"And here we go." Lorcan sighed and stood up, rushing to the kitchen to aid his dad and escape the madness. Hey, even his patience had limitations.

"I am not mean. And my cat knows it!"

"You are too! Otherwise, where is she?"

"Wicked? That cat is as insane as you, old woman. Whether or not I said anything mean to her is beside the point—which I did not—Wicked is no delicate flower."

"Where is she then?"

"That's what I'm trying to find out!"

"Well, shouting about it isn't going to help!"

"I'm not shouting. Much. Argh!"

I threw my arms into the air and myself into the closest unoccupied armchair and began tugging at my long mane. Just then, my dad, Charlie, and my mom, Adelaide, came through the back door and stopped short.

"What on Earth happened to the kitchen. Lily, dear, did you try to make something?"

Gee, the vote of confidence from my own parents—or lack thereof—stung pretty badly.

"All I did was try to fix the coffee machine."

"Oh! Is it broken? I could have gotten you one at Walmart this morning," said Charlie, trying to be helpful. Ever since my dad returned to us, he'd been desperately trying to make up for lost time, make amends for his absence, which he insisted was his fault—it was not. He even began taking my mom on dates and wooing her even though they'd been married well over twenty-seven years now—although most of them were spent apart.

"It's not broken. Not now."

"Um...OK. But..."

"It's not broken because when Lily let loose her amazing display of horrific magic, the coffee machine began to work once more, but the kitchen went BOOM!" said Andrea, trying to be helpful. It was not helpful. Not to me, anyway.

"Oh dear." Adelaide looked mournfully in my direction, and I knew my dad was trying hard to keep the positive look on his face—he was failing miserably. Twenty-two years being apart, the last thing he wanted to do was seem disappointed in his failure of a witch daughter.

"And now she's lost her cat."

I turned to Adriana and crooked my finger at her nose. "Listen, you old bat. You should be more worried about pissing me off—all things considered—and not have me lob a spell in your direction!"

"Pshaw."

"Oh really?"

"Yes, really. Like I can't handle a pup like you with a broken wand and half my medications not taken."

"Oh, so you finally admit you take drugs. Dementia? Hardening of the arteries?" I'd poked at her for over a year now, threatening to have her locked up for her erratic behavior. Give me an inch—and admittance she was on some kind of pills—and I would be all over it in seconds.

"It's to keep me calm, so I don't zap ungrateful brats."

"Aha! Mental illness. I knew it."

Andrea and Pandora had been watching Adriana and I go back and forth with some mild amusement, but now they slunk away in unison, assuming one or both of us would start lobbing spells back and forth as promised. It could happen. Had happened.

With spectacular results...it even left a few scars around town before my great-grandfather Antonio fixed them with magic.

Eileen was peering around the kitchen cabinet she held open for Henry's examination and Lorcan was facing away from us, but his shoulders were rocking, so I knew he was amused. I think he secretly liked my spunk, and how I stood up to Adriana. Of course, he'd never admit it...especially not to her face.

Edith chose that moment to swirl away in a puff of smoke and ectoplasm.

"Liliana. I'm going to let that one pass because I know you are upset about your cat and the Witch Council. However, you don't seem to realize just how much trouble you are in. Otherwise, I think you'd be quite a bit more subdued than you are."

Charlie and Adelaide glanced at each other, then tracked their eyes to Adriana. My mother came to kneel beside me and grabbed both my hands in hers.

"Lily. Please, baby. I know how frustrating all of this is. But fighting with your great-grandmother won't solve anything."

No, but it made me feel better. That counted for something.

I'd like to say I remained calm and mature. I'd like to say I lowered my voice and argued my point like an adult. Heck, I'd like to say I sat there and refused to say another word. I'd like to say any of those things, but unfortunately I can't. Because what I did even shocked Adriana, and that old witch doesn't shock easily, let me tell you.

What did I go and do to my utter embarrassment? I

opened my mouth to argue but instead a sob came out. Then I began to wail like a banshee!

"I just want to get married, have a bunch of little Lorcans, and be able to walk around town using magic without everyone running away in fear! Is that too much to ask?"

It didn't help my cause that at that exact moment, the coffee maker made a loud popping sound and began to smoke.

Et tu Mr. Coffee?

"Now, look. Your kitchen is sparkling. Everything is fixed—including the coffee maker—and Henry isn't too worse for wear. Try to put a smile on your face, honey. Everything will work out. I know it will."

Charlie Sweet was trying his best with me. I will give him that. But after all these years apart, I felt entitled to throwing a massive sulk-fest and no cajoling on his part would get me out of my funk. I knew I was being a baby—I just didn't care. My dad patted me on the shoulder and gave it a little squeeze before returning to my mother's side.

Just then, Molly Hogan, my friend and a trusted human came into the kitchen from the yard. Her hair was disheveled, and she looked frantic yet charming at the same time, and I just couldn't quite figure out how she managed to pull it off every time. Molly had been living with me ever since her boyfriend, Ted, was murdered—a long, sad tale—and she decided to remain in Georgia instead of going back to her hometown of Asheville.

She'd recently taken the apartment over June's Emporium, the store named for a dear family friend, and the place I'd once stayed when I first moved to town.

"Lily! Oh my gosh, you need to leave, and be quick

about it."

"Hi to you too, Molly," drawled Pandora. Dorie hadn't taken a shining to my friend, and I threw her a look as if to say, "quit it."

"What?" Dorie tried to look innocent, but she wasn't fooling me. She didn't fool Molly either, but the former chose to ignore the poor behavior and remained focused on me.

"Lily, I mean it. I just came from Brian's cruiser. He just happened to be passing by when I left the diner and offered me a ride." This was a blatant lie on Molly's part because we all knew Brian didn't go around picking up women who were walking from the diner and driving them to the Emporium—a short, diagonal walk across the street on the opposite side. No. Brian and Molly were sweet on each other but for some reason were desperately trying to hide the fact. Everyone thought it was adorable.

I found it annoying.

But then again, I found everything annoying as of late.

"Molly, slow down. Why do I need to leave?"

"Brian's phone went off, and I heard a one-sided conversation but pieced enough of it together to know you are in trouble. Like big trouble."

"What did I do now? I've been sitting here all morning!" Blowing up my house and sending unpredictable magic loose wherever I pointed my fingers. That's all. Nothing to see.

"Word reached the Witch Council about a little incident here this morning?" Molly spoke in questions, and I began to feel a headache creeping in. "And someone there is on the warpath? Didn't your Uncle Owen call and warn you?"

"Yes, but..."

"Well, apparently something big is going down, and Sheriff Buford called Brian and told him not to get involved and, oh, Lily. You need to run because the cops are on their way to arrest you!"

"What?!" I felt my peaceful weekend plans dwindling by the second.

I wasn't the only one to shout that question at the top of their lungs. Both my parents, Lorcan, and Adriana were equally shocked. Henry Reid was so shocked, his dentures popped out of his mouth—again. Eileen was crying softy and clutching a tissue. Andrea was angrily protesting on my behalf, hands on her hips and shoulders squared. But then we heard the telltale sound of tires on my gravel driveway, and I knew the jig was up.

That's what they say, right? I didn't know who *they* were, but right now they were screaming inside my head to run!

I stood and scrambled to the kitchen window, horrified when my eyes landed on the two patrol cars outside and Sweet Briar's finest heading in my direction. Without even a backward glance at my family, I grabbed my phone and the keys to my car and flew toward the front door, not even stopping to think, despite hearing their protests.

I couldn't worry about that now. I needed to get out of here before they nabbed me. I had a cat to find, and no Witch Council would stop me from doing just that. Throwing open the door even as I could hear my family greet the sheriff, I wasn't paying much attention, which was why I found myself running smack into the last person I wanted to see right then.

Deputy Tiffany Clarkson, of the Sweet Briar Clarksons was all business, bedecked in her police finery, shiny blonde hair pulled back into a severe ponytail. She didn't even smirk when she slapped a band around my wrist, instantly nullifying my magic and said, "Lily Sweet, you have the right to remain silent. Anything you do or say may be held against you in the Witch Court of Law."

Nope. Not going to have that peaceful weekend any time soon it seems!

3

Do you have any idea how humiliating it is to be carted off to jail in the back of a police cruiser in front of all of your neighbors and friends? It has to be right up there with almost burning down the town one year or having a fight in front of the funeral home where it was shouted out loud that I was in the market for a threesome. I was not.

I don't think the town believed it.

Much.

Not even those incidents could compare to the drive around the square and being paraded into the police station by the hated Deputy Clarkson, while my family argued and trailed behind in our wake with the entire town out and standing in shocked attention at the haphazard parade of lunatics. Oh, and do not doubt they were going all-out nuts. It looked like a parade of insanity, complete with marching bands and floats.

Gordy Polk stopped his garbage truck in the middle of the road, he was in such a state. Joe came out of his kitchen and stood in the big picture window of his diner with Sheila, his waitress and Gordy's spouse, by his side. The not-so-new waitress didn't bother joining them—I wasn't particularly friendly with her, nor could I recall her name. The times I went to the diner she was either off or heading out.

Chester and Hester Soule—rhymes with ghoul—the brother and sister duo who ran said funeral home, stood agog on the sidewalk with Hermione and Hortense Winters...the witchy sisters who ran the tearoom. This was astounding since the Soules and Winters had an ongoing feud and my passing by caused a temporary cease-fire that I alone deemed miraculous.

Chester waved at me sadly, almost like he already knew they'd finally throw away the key once my sorry behind was in a prison cell.

Becky Nolan was in the doorway of her bookstore, on her cell phone, and I suspected she was calling her boyfriend, and my attorney, Jake Carter...June, of the Emporium's son. Speaking of June, she was on the sidewalk with her husband Dennis and employee Maureen Kennedy. Now, Maureen, *she* had a big, huge, grin on her face...and who could blame her? She hated me, and this little display had to be the best thing going for her considering she was a pocked-faced, dishwater blonde with a fondness for Twinkies.

Catty, yes, I know. I tend to lose any sense of decency where Maureen is concerned. Bullies bring out the worst in me, and Maureen is a bully—or thinks she is, anyway. She certainly terrorizes her peers and those in the younger set. But when she gets out of hand, my darling cat, Wicked, always seems to manage to bring her down a peg or two.

Even Rita Chase, Brian's mother, and her new employee, Terri, stood outside their shops and watched in bemused amazement as my entire family marched *loudly* into the police station and demanded an explanation.

Abner, my handyman, all recovered from a recent ankle break, was shaking his head with worry beside Stu, Lorcan's mechanic, and our town's mayor. Perhaps he could step in and clear up this nonsense, but I suspected his title of mayor was an honorary one because I've yet to see him preside over anything of importance. But what did I know?

As for me? I was over it. I wanted a nap. Or full-out hibernation. In a cave, down the hollow, over the ridge into North Carolina, besides a gently rolling stream—preferably a few counties away from our border. Heck, they could throw me in a cell and toss away the key as far as I was concerned, as long as I had a cot and a soft pillow. Did they even have pillows in prison? No. I don't care. I'm done. Over it. Finished.

"I'm going to need you to follow me into this room and strip."

Wait. What?

❀

"I've been violated."

"Lily, no one violated you. Tiffany was just kidding."

"I still had to have that wand probe thing come at me," I grumbled.

"No one probed you, Lily. They just waved it up and down and around to make sure you aren't carrying any magical items on your person," said Lorcan, patiently.

"Like what? Eye of newt? Bat wings? Who does that anyway? I have a roll of Lifesavers in my pocket You better be careful—they may go off!"

Lorcan sighed softly. I knew he was trying to calm me down and make things better, but at this point I was livid and irrational.

"And this nullifying band," I cried, holding my arm up, "How insulting is this? Like what? I'm going to zap everyone I see with dark magic and morph into this rampaging lunatic?

How can the Council, half of whom are supposed to be family and or friends, think this of me? It's insulting, and quite frankly, leaves me unable to trust anyone in this town any longer!"

I huffed and threw myself down on the cot—yes, it had a pillow, but it left much to be desired. In some areas, it was totally flat like a pancake, while in others it was lumpy. I'd not get a moment's rest on that any time soon.

"Lily, have faith that Jake and your Uncle Owen are working on this. Judge Owen, being who he is, cannot preside on this matter...but for some reason, Judge Dietrich likes you —despite his family. He won't be swayed one way or the other. Jake is securing your release right now. This was just a preliminary move by those who feel you are a threat...but they don't have ground to stand on when it comes to you and your character. You will be out soon enough."

Like that was supposed to make me feel better. Hint...it didn't.

"Let me go see what the holdup is. Look, here's Adriana to keep you company."

Great. She's probably here to torture me while I'm help- less and incarcerated...and unable to threaten her with my amazing disastrous magical fingers. She'd probably spend my last moments before I'm transported to prison cackling at me or telling me she'd expected this all along. I'm a failure, useless, a basic witch of little use.

"Hey, Squirt. Don't you look woebegone? It will be OK, dear, don't fret."

Fine. So, she wasn't cackling—yet.

"Wouldn't you?"

"Not really. Jail suits me. It gives you street cred."

"Street cred. What are you? A gangster?" I sniffed.

"I could be, smartass. I'm one bad witch."

"Yeah, yeah. Meanwhile, I'm stuck in here. My cat is still

missing, and I can't go out there and look for her, and I've become a pariah and someone to avoid. Life is forever changed for me, and I might as well leave Sweet Briar, if they ever let me out of prison, that is."

Yes, I was laying it on thick. I was miserable and chilled, and wanted my big, soft bed.

"Such drama! Listen, Liliana. Things seem bleak now, but we've got this. My time with the Order of Origin gave me some insight as to what is going on behind the scenes." Adriana was more subdued than I'd ever seen her, and it gave me pause. What could be so dire to cause this change in attitude?

"What is it?"

"Now before you fly off the handle when I tell you, you must understand the rules have been changing for years now and things are getting better for some..."

Adriana trailed off, and I became uneasy. This was definitely unlike her, and I knew, whatever she'd say next, would not only upset me, but probably cause me to explode. I immediately prepared myself, making the resolution to remain calm no matter what.

"It's Tarni Vanderzee. The Order is hunting her, Liliana. Things...well, things are changing...again."

"What?! Hunting her? They can't. Tarni isn't a criminal! What do you mean, 'hunting her?' Are they out of their minds? She's a peaceful mermaid living at the bottom of a pond for heaven's sake!"

So much for remaining calm. But we are talking about my siren friend—cousin, actually—and I promised Tarni I'd keep those who might bring trouble to her doorstep at bay.

"Hang on...is she still here? At Nichol's Pond? We have to warn her!"

"No, Liliana. I'm not sure where she is, nor did I offer any opinions to these hounds chasing her. But you have to understand something about Tarni that might alter your opinion. You see, she's done some things in her lifetime that she should be lauded for...but other things? She has brutally murdered some people, who may or may not have deserved it —but without any authority, she has always been considered a dangerous renegade."

"That's balderdash!"

Adriana smiled slightly at my heated response.

"Your loyalty is admirable, dear. But Tarni knew full well what she was doing and unfortunately, her past is coming back to haunt her...or in her case...hunt her. The Order of Origin cannot overlook these charges. We've had peace among the Breed and many dangerous aspects of our kind have been impelled to change toward the better. Vampires no longer prey on humans for instance, but have willing hosts, witches don't go around using vile magic for ill-gotten gains, demons are kept in check...unless one is a renegade. Hence your situation and why you are being analyzed so."

"But that's hogwash, and you know it! I'm no renegade!"

"Liliana! I know it, most of the Witch Council know it, even some at the Order of Origin—your cousin Maggie as a matter of fact, know it. But others? Those here who want trouble for our family? Those in the Order who do not know us and have only seen what has been going on this past year and a half...and my kin, Lucretia, causing so much harm. Naturally, they are focused on you and have questions. Especially now as they've discovered you are a sweet briar witch."

"But forget about me for a minute. What is going to happen to Tarni?" I wailed, my voice cracking in worry and filled with trepidation.

"Your concern is most admirable. It is one of the things I love most about you, my dear. Your compassion and loyalty." Adriana smiled sadly at me and continued. "I don't know what will become of Tarni. If they find her...it won't be good.

I pray she has resources to keep her hidden and safe. But right now, my concern is you, and getting you out of here."

"She can do that any time she wants." Jake Carter walked in at that moment with a huge grin on his face. "Judge Dietrich came through, despite heavy protestations from Wilhelmina. Lily is free to go under one condition. No magic until further notice."

"Preposterous! But what can we do?" Adriana barked.

"Do? We fight! That's what we do! I need to clear my name and stop those who would harm Tarni."

"Um...not going to happen, Lily. You need to stay away from anything to do with that siren," Jake scolded.

"That *siren* is part of me...or I am part of her. We are kin! I won't let any harm come to her if I can help it and that's a promise! Jake, I gave Tarni my word I'd aid her if and when those hunting her came looking. What am I supposed to do —ignore the fact that she's in danger?"

"You are to do just that, Lily. Stay out of it."

I growled and stomped my foot in frustration but remained quiet despite my feelings on the subject. Things needed to change in our world in a hurry. I needed to clear my name, get back on the Council, and become a force to be reckoned with. Somehow, I suspected my sudden incarceration and the need to put me on trial had more to do with poor Tarni and less to do with my errant magic. Someone powerful learned of our friendship in some way and wants me out of the picture.

We shall just see about that!

❦ 4 ❧

Monday morning dawned bright and early, and while I relished my freedom, I still had no Wicked. I was beyond frantic at this point and decided I'd go out and about around town and look for her—despite my loathing having everyone ask questions about my current situation. Wicked trumped my need to hide away from the world. Maybe I could knock on some doors and ask my friends and neighbors if they'd seen her. Someone had to...she's almost as infamous as I am!

Edith promised to wander in and among the neighbors' homes and yards in an attempt to find her, but I had my doubts she would find Wicked in any of them...although I appreciated her offer. No, this was something I needed to do in the hopes that she'd moved out of her usual haunts and branched out further.

I trudged up Wildflower Lane, my street, then turned right on Main and headed to the square. My first stop was Rita Chase's Mystic Fox metaphysical store and her Fox Den Herbals next door. She'd recently hired Ted and Tommy Gruber's aunt as her new herbal expert, and Terri Parks has been a godsend. Rita had been trying to run both shops by herself ever since her old employee, Samantha Fairburn, turned out to be a murderous shrew—aunt to the missing diabolical teen, Rowan Nightingale, and best buds with the insane Fredricks sisters. I knew the entire town hoped Terri would be a calm and capable herbalist—with no crazy hidden secrets in her closet. So far, so good.

"Hello, Lily. I haven't seen you in here in quite some time. Well, except for a few minutes the other day." Rita Chase was a gorgeous auburn-haired witch with her son Brian's eyes. Striking and rather imposing at times, we were finally getting back to a friendly relationship after some misunderstandings —or rather, we chose to ignore some of the things that had come up to cause an awkward wedge in our relationship and move on. Her mild chiding was to be expected, and I tried not to let it get under my skin.

"Hi, Rita. How are things?"

"Wonderful. Terri is doing splendidly, and I am thinking of making her a full partner."

Wow, Terri Parks must really know her herbs to have Rita considering something so monumental.

"Oh, that's awesome, Rita. I know you've been stretched thin."

"So what brings you here?" Rita said this just as Terri came in from the shop next door and gave me a little wave.

"Well, you see, Wicked is missing, and I wonder if you've seen her around town?"

"Wicked is Lily's gorgeous black cat." Rita addressed this to Terri who nodded in understanding, a worried frown on her face.

"Have you asked around, posted notices?"

"Not yet. That's what I'm doing today...asking people if they've seen her. It's not like she's a normal cat...and even they tend to be smart and can find their way home. Wicked is special, magical, so I'm worried because where could she be...

and why take off without letting me know in some way? It's not like her!"

"Have you called the pound?" Terri asked.

"We have a pound?"

"No, we have a no-kill shelter...but if someone picked her up, they may have taken her to the one in Rabun County," said Rita.

Oh no! Why did I not think of this?

I thanked the women and rushed out of the shop and onto the street where I whipped out my phone and began calling everyone who might have my cat. The shelter, the pound, even my vet. No one had a highly intelligent black cat, nor did they get one in in the last few days. Where on earth is Wicked?

I began trudging along and found myself outside June's Emporium. Peering through the windows, I could see Molly at the counter speaking with June and breathed a sigh of relief—no Maureen in sight.

"Hey, guys."

"Lily! Oh, my dear...how horrible for you. I felt so helpless when I saw what happened on Saturday," cried June, rushing over to embrace me.

"Yeah, well...there is nothing like a little arrest to liven things up around here."

"Lily don't be so flip about it. I would have about died if the police came for me!" Molly lamented .

"Par for the course when it comes to me, lately. It's OK, Molly. Jake came to my rescue, and all is well...for now."

"Well, I am certainly glad Jake set them straight." June said this proudly, and I knew she was beyond proud of her son. "Let's just hope no more ridiculous allegations pop up from a certain group in this town."

"What do you mean?" I asked.

"Those Dietrichs and Langsfords have been stirring up a

campaign of trouble for you. My brother told me all about it."
Her brother being my uncle by marriage, Judge Owen
Haywood. He is married to my Aunt Iona, my mom's sister.

"Well, they can stir all they want. I refuse to let them
rattle me. What's more, I've decided I need to go on the
attack. Do you know right at this minute the Order of Origin
is hunting my friend, Tarni?"

June's demeanor changed in an instant, and I grew
suspicious.

"Well, Lily, dear, she isn't someone who I'd expect would
survive long with all the horrible things she is purported to
have done. I'm surprised it took the Order this long to
pinpoint her location."

"June! How can you say that? Tarni is related to me! She
helped us when we needed it by giving me some of her tears!
She is my friend!"

Molly looked shaken, and I tried to tone down my anger.

"I don't understand much about renegades and the history
from the past. I just know the person I met recently...Tarni is
good people."

"If you say so, Lily. I didn't mean to upset you." June
seemed chastised, so I gave her a hug to apologize further.

"I'm sorry for shouting, June. I'm on edge. You see,
Wicked is missing and..."

"Wicked! Oh no! But she was just here!"

"What? What do you mean?" I cried.

"She came for her usual breakfast this morning and
seemed fine. Did someone snatch her?"

"Wait! What? This morning? June! She has been missing
since Wednesday. Do you mean to tell me that lousy cat has
been coming here for a visit?"

"Every morning like clockwork," replied June.

How do you like that? Wicked isn't missing. She's avoiding

me...or worse. She decided to move out and how do you like them apples? That ungrateful beast!

With a lump in my throat, I mumbled my goodbyes to June and Molly and asked June to call me should Wicked show up again. Although, what good would that do if Wicked wanted no part of me? I begrudgingly admitted to myself I loved that persnickety cat, but if it isn't reciprocated and she hates me...what was the point of trying to find her?

Perhaps I should just go home and wallow in self-pity. I mean, if my cat doesn't want to live with me anymore...if she took off and remained in town to visit my friends...why bother searching for her? She obviously doesn't want me to find her, or she wouldn't have left in the first place. I'm grateful she is OK, but I won't go looking for a cat who obviously has wiped her hands—paws—of her mistress.

Sour much?

You betcha!

5

"We need a plan, Lil."

Pandora was lounging on my sofa in the den when I arrived home, eating an ice cream pop. Several popsicle sticks were strewn about with a few empty boxes.

"Just how many of these have you eaten?" I asked.

"Enough that she should be buzzing with a sugar high by now," Edith sniffed. She was sulking across the room perched on a chair nearest the sunporch...although it was difficult to tell since her lower half was missing.

"Huh? Oh, these? I don't know. Three? Seven? Anyway...I think we need to go on the offensive. Shake the Council up a little and take charge of your situation. Then we need to do something about that skank."

"Skank? Oh, Tiffany. Yeah...well, I'm done worrying about her."

"Oh really? Did you know I passed the shop early this morning when Lorcan arrived, and her brand new window shade just happened to come crashing down right as she was lathering up in her shower? I thought Stu was about to have a heart attack. But Lorcan? He just stood there staring at ole

Tiff like she was a juicy steak, and he was just off a hunger strike."

"Mm hmm...and I saw them in her yard yesterday going over that ridiculous rabbit hutch, even though her rabbit has been missing for quite some time now," said Edith.

What?

"Dorie, are you sure? Edith? Please don't lay this on me right now on top of the Council issues and the fact my cat hates me and has run away from home!" I wailed.

"Wicked ran away from home?"

"Yes! June said she's been visiting her every morning for breakfast but where has she been around here? Gone. Missing. Poof. I guess she doesn't love me anymore. And it sounds like she isn't the only one."

"Lily Sweet. Don't you dare think that about Lorcan. He can't help himself. He's a man. They see boobies and all sense leaves their brains," cried Edith.

"Boobies. Heh," snickered Pandora. "What Lily needs is a bit of Pandora-style mischief. Shake things up. Turn everyone on their head. Roll the dice and see what comes of it. Sometimes, the best kind of magic happens when the unexpected becomes reality because those that matter are all on the same page. I need to show you how to make that kind of magic, Lily. Especially since your boobies aren't as magnificent as Tiffany's." Dorie and Edith giggled, but I scowled.

I didn't find anything funny enough to laugh about. I growled a little and threw my handbag down onto the kitchen table and joined Pandora and Edith in my den. "I call bull. I'm sorry, but that's not a good excuse. If he loved me, he wouldn't have remained transfixed on Tiffany Clarkson. At all. Dorie, Edith...my entire world is falling apart."

"Oh, please! Why would he bother to write your names in that magical marriage book you witches have if he didn't want to marry you?"

34

Over the Christmas holiday, not only had Lorcan and I decided on a marriage date, but we'd also sneakily written down our names in the magical marriage banns book...sealing the deal, so to speak. But if he was mesmerized by the magnificent mammaries of a malevolent blonde mean girl...what chance did I have at a happy life with him?

"Perhaps he's a big, dumb, jerk and has been one all along and I'm a bad judge of character and he intends to wed me but play around behind my back! I'm not doing this. I can't handle any more drama and intrigue...and... who the heck is that?"

Drawing my attention away from my plight, I found myself gazing at the strange visage of an unkempt person. Standing outside my sunporch window was a bedraggled-looking man swaying back and forth, holding a sack in one hand and a Walmart bag in the other. He was peering in my window with a vacant look in his eyes. His clothing seemed frayed and worn with dirty patches to match the smudge on his face. He looked like he'd been living outside for some time.

"Where? Oh! Huh...he looks homeless."

Edith flew through the wall and hovered over the man then turned to us and shrugged like she couldn't make out why he was standing outside my home.

Dorie and I walked to my back door and went out onto my porch. Then we trudged around the side of my house until we reached the area on the outside of my sunporch where the man had been standing. The area was clear and a few seconds of looking had us discovering his whereabouts. The man had moved to my porch steps around front and was shuffling around, looking down at the ground as if searching for something he'd lost.

"Can I help you?"

35

The man jerked his head up, spying us both, then dropped his Walmart bag and ran off up my street toward Main Street.

"Hey! Hang on a minute. You dropped your bag!"

Taking off after the man, Dorie and I managed to over-take him just as he reached the corner near Carter's Hard-ware and Rita's shops before coming to the square. Dennis Carter and Donald Murphy, owner of the motel on the outskirts of town were standing in front of the hardware store and saw us approaching. They came over to where we stopped the man, Pandora holding fast to his sleeve with Edith flying around throwing punches.

I wanted to swat her away, and she must have caught my annoying glance and shake of my head, because she stopped her shenanigans and dissolved into nothingness. Great. Now I've gone and upset Edith.

"Here, you dropped this. Why were you in my yard? Are you hungry?"

"Evil witch! Let go of me! Evil, darkness...bad. Bad!" Spittle flew out of his mouth and eyes wild with fear began rolling back in his head.

The frightened man began to back away from me, stum-bling a little in his haste to distance himself. By this point, June and Molly had come outside and so had Rita and Terri. I even noticed Becky across the square standing with my friend Martha who ran the library. Everyone was concerned but not overly so...at least they knew I wasn't an evil dark witch, like this man was claiming—or so I hoped.

"Listen, buddy. I just came to bring you back your bag. You were the one wandering around my yard."

"Evil. Evil dark witch. They need to burn you. BURN!"

What the heck? I'd had enough at this point and thrust the bag at the man, fully intending on turning and heading back to my home, washing my hands of this nonsense. But that's when he reached out to grab the bag and everything went to hell in a hurry. KABLOOEY!

❀

"I didn't do a thing! No magic, no thoughts of magic. One minute I was handing the guy his bag and the next, things were blowing up like a smoke bomb went off. But I had nothing to do with it!"

I could not believe my luck—or lack of it.

"Did anyone see what happened?" Sheriff Buford was kneeling on the pavement, snapping photos with his phone, the paramedics already having come and gone to rush the hapless man to the hospital. When the bag exploded, the homeless man took the full brunt of whatever it was that went off and down he went, hitting the pavement with a thud.

"Are you serious? The entire town was outside watching. As a matter of fact, they're all still here with a few more stragglers coming out to see what all the fuss is about!" I cried.

"That's just dandy, Lily. But I meant did anyone see what you did or did not do?" he replied.

Oh.

Well, then.

"It looked like Lily was handing him a plastic bag, and then there was a loud bang and flash...unfortunately, it all happened so quickly, I couldn't see exactly what happened," said Dennis. Donald nodded his head in agreement.

"And you two were the closest?"

"Yes. We came to see if Lily needed any aid. The old guy was acting weird, frothing at the mouth, eyes rolled back and was saying some nasty things to our Lily here," said Donald. Good egg, that man.

"Yeah? Like what?"

"Oh, um, that she was evil and, uh, needed to be burned or something, not that, well..."

Sheriff Buford sat back on his heels and squinted up at me, giving me an assessing look before sighing and shaking his head. "Must it always be you when these things happen?"

Seriously? Who else would it be? He needn't have bothered asking, even I knew I was the bad luck witch in this town.

"Hey! All I did was give the homeless man his bag. He was in my yard poking around, acting all weird and creepy. He ran off when we confronted him but it was he who decided looking in my windows was a good idea. I didn't ask him to enter my yard! I'm the victim here...well, sort of. I didn't let any magic out. Don't you believe me?"

"Lily, it isn't a matter of me believing you, it's a matter of..."

"Arrest her Sheriff. Now. We cannot have this renegade witch continue to terrorize this town and our fine citizens with her capricious, unstable magic." The voice of Wilhelmina Dietrich reached my ears before I saw her approaching, all puffed up and dripping in mink and jewels. And here I thought the old witch had thawed a bit toward me. I guess not.

"Oh look! Here comes that old blowhard with wrinkled stockings. You'd think with *her* money she'd be able to buy some that didn't pool around her rather wide ankles."

"Not now, Dorie!" Great...just what I needed. Pandora and Wilhelmina going at it in the street with the sheriff watching. Edith frowned at Wilhelmina, her grandmother, then slowly faded from sight.

"Now see here. Lily did nothing to that man! I was standing right beside her and from what I could see that bag just burst into a kaleidoscope of color," argued Donald.

Of course, you'd stick up for her! You're under her spell it seems! Bewitched by a renegade," chided Wilhelmina, wagging her finger under Donald's nose.

"How can he be under my spell, you dingbat? Either I'm a renegade witch with wonky magic as you claim, or I'm what? A skilled temptress? You can't have it both ways, Wilma!"

"How dare you! Impudent child." Wilhelmina drew herself up in righteous indignation, especially since I used the name my great-grandmother often teased her nemesis with. Speaking of which, the screeching tires and giant sedan that came barreling around the corner and skidded to a stop at the curb in front of us, held none other than Adriana Dolce. And she was livid.

For once I was happy to see my granny show up guns blazing, although I wondered at the car. It wasn't my granny's old green Lincoln Town Car. This was silver and newer, and I wasn't quite sure of the model.

"What is the meaning of this, Sheriff Buford? I was having a pleasant repast with Antonio when I receive a frantic call from our dear friend Becky Nolan only to find out my great-granddaughter is being harassed by this puffed-up hen once more!"

"Now, Adriana. No one is harassing Lily. I just have some questions for her is all."

"Wilhelmina is harassing her!" This from Dennis Carter.

"It's more like she's bleating like a goat, but none of us is really listening—we just like watching that vein on her head bulge out and wonder if she'll stroke out if she gets agitated enough," sniggered Pandora, throwing an evil grin in Wilhelmina's direction.

"Dorie!"

"What?"

"Wilma needs to explain how she just happened to be here when this little occurrence went down, throwing accusations at my kin. Especially since I know for a fact she was at the Witch Council not fifteen minutes ago speaking in hushed tones on her cellphone before urgently whispering some nonsense about, 'we have her now. This time it won't be so easy to spring her out of jail.'"

Wilhelmina blanched, and her mouth opened and closed a few times before she managed to regain her composure. "I said no such thing. How would you even know where I was? Or what I said!"

"Because I have people watching you, Wilma. Don't you think I know you're behind this campaign to unseat my family? I'd be a fool not to keep tabs on you!"

Wilhelmina looked upset, angry, and chagrined at the same time and gazed shrewdly at my great-grandmother. "Well, I never! I did no such thing!"

"Oh really? Jared!" hollered Adriana, snapping her fingers toward the silver vehicle.

I scrunched up my face trying to figure out if Adriana was going mental or if someone was sitting unnoticed in said vehicle. But that's when the car began to shimmer in ways that made me somewhat queasy, then morphed into a tallish man with silver blonde hair and gleaming white teeth. He was smiling profusely and bowed slightly before addressing my great-grandmother, leaving Wilhelmina speechless.

"At your command, Adriana."

"Please show the sheriff what you recorded on your cell phone."

"As you wish."

This Jared is a shifter—I mean, what else could he be? Ten seconds ago, he had four tires and a trunk! He began flicking through his phone's photographs until he came up with a video recording of Wilhelmina at the Council doing and saying exactly what Adriana had claimed.

The sputtering and protestations died on Wilhelmina's

lips and a cold demeanor slid down her face, making her appear to be carved from marble.

"Now how much do you want to bet old Wilma here had something to do with this entire farce? Maybe she hired that man, and this was one more attempt to frame my great-granddaughter!"

"I did not! I have my own people out and about. I will have you know that the paramedic is a family friend and he called me to tell me what occurred. You can just wipe that grin off your face, Adriana. Your great-granddaughter is a menace! I hope that poor unfortunate sues you for everything you are worth!"

"That poor unfortunate won't be doing much of anything anymore." Sheriff Buford disconnected from the call he'd been on, unbeknownst to us, and sighed once more. "That was the hospital. The man just died. I don't know if we are dealing with a horrible accident or murder, but I do know one thing—no one is leaving this town, no witch anyway, until I have this thing solved. And you, Lily, are to remain home for the foreseeable future or I will throw you in jail and toss the key myself."

❦ 6 ❧

Of course, the Sheriff's proclamation meant Pandora and I were on the road bright and early the next day, despite knowing we'd definitely both get tossed in the new prison and never see the light of day if Glen Buford discovered our downright insubordination. Although we hadn't left town, I was certain he'd blow a gasket if he knew I was out and about and not home like he'd ordered. But despite knowing better, I found myself agreeing to doing things Dorie's way for once.

It started last night when we convened to discuss the day's occurrences, and I quickly lost any argument contrary to her ideas.

It ended when, bleary eyed and sleep deprived, I agreed that perhaps doing things my way...or the way I've been doing them, might not be the way to go any longer. I mean, Dorie seems to always manage to come out ahead, surprise me, and get the job done—so why fight her?

Either I've lost my mind completely or I've learned to trust my instincts and my demon friend...and right now? Pandora's kind of chaos was what I needed in my life.

It was game on—Dorie style.

"What is it exactly that we're doing?" I asked her for the tenth time.

"Lily. We need to shake things up in the Witch Council. You need to assert your rights and take what has been yours all along. Your great-grandfather on down helped build that Council up to what it is today. This town, every success, everything, is due to him, Adriana, and your family in general. We are going to come up with something so amazeballs, the entire place—from the lowliest novice witch to the collective Elders will get their comeuppance. It's time you demanded your birthright and run this town!"

"Sounds like a plan...but, gosh, Dorie... I have no plan! I entered the Council, took a position, and thought I had a platform, but they pulled the rug out from under me before I could make any waves. All I ever got out of it was that I wanted to tackle Breed reform."

"That's what you have me for, kiddo. Trust me, by the time I'm done with them, every last member of the Witch Council will see reason and you will once again be a card-carrying member with wedding bells in your future."

I certainly hoped so, but right now I had to get over the fact that my benefactress was donning a skintight green miniskirt, had decided to add blood red tips to her hair, had five-inch stiletto boots on and had a bow and arrow strapped to her back. Well, she did until we got in my Jeep, and she placed it on the back seat.

It also didn't help that she opted for a see-through mesh top and forgot to put on a bra this morning until I pointed out that not only was her outfit unacceptable for obvious reasons, but it was also finally cold enough that her—ahem—upper region, might be able to cut glass if she went out dressed as such in the cold. Dorie shrugged and trudged up the stairs only to return with a fuzzy black bra on—over the mesh top—and a long woolen cardigan that looked like something Lara Croft would find kinky.

My life was truly bizarre.

"Where and when do you think Adriana hooked up with that Jared dude?" Pandora asked, popping her bubble gum and combing through her hair before twisting it up in two long pigtails. Great. Now she looked like an alternate, even more demented version of Harley Quinn from DC comics.

"I don't know. And she took off so quickly after Sheriff Buford told us we could go I didn't get a chance to grill her. He's positively dreamy though in a Nordic male model, shifter dude, slightly off mentally, serial killer kind of way. I mean, that's his vibe anyway—with heaps of charm and guile. I felt like running to Lorcan to beg forgiveness for my girl parts reacting so strongly to that guy's visage. I think he's dangerous."

"Oh, he's dangerous alright. He's an assassin of some kind, or I'm not a crossroads demon. And yes. I noticed him right away. He's the kind of man that makes your father stay up at night worrying that you're on a date with a lady-killer to end all lady-killers. Well, he can slay me anytime! Rowr!"

I giggled, and it felt good. Somewhere along the way, Pandora became a friend and ally, and it felt right trusting her plan, even though I still had no idea what that was right this minute.

"Do I even want to know what you have up your sleeve?"

"I think it might be better to trust I have things well in hand and leave it there," replied Dorie.

"Oh? And why is that?" I asked with some apprehension.

"Well, for one thing, I know where Wicked has been hanging out, and you're not going to like it or understand. And two...we're heading there after we make a little stop first."

"What? What do you mean...how...when...how come you know where she is, and I don't?"

"Breathe, Lily."

"Don't you tell me to breathe! How long have you known where Wicked has been? And why would it upset me? Wait. Is she OK? Does she not want to live with me anymore?"

I felt my lower lip tremble with emotions that I fought to keep inside. I didn't want to start blubbering over the fact that I was hurt far more than I'd let on about Wicked's defection.

"Slow down, sugar! My goodness, but you get so needy! Wicked hasn't left you, silly. She's been on a fact-finding mission and just sent word that it's time to spring into action."

How on earth did Wicked and Dorie communicate? Did I even want to know? And a fact-finding mission? What was she? A ninja cat?

"Where are we going right now?" I asked, hating the pouty sound of my voice.

"Right now, we are going to see a man about a book—well, a vampire man, anyway."

Oh, goody. Let's go see a... wait. Hang on just a minute!

"Mortimer! Pandora...you could have told me we were coming to see Mortimer and not freak me out so!" I chided.

"Where's the fun in that?" Pandora hopped out of my Jeep, took a few teetering steps in Mortimer's direction and promptly fell on her face, skidding a few feet before stopping.

Great. Dorie forgot to put on underwear too, it seems.

"Oopsie!"

"Mortimer, help Dorie up. Dorie, cut that out...you can't straighten your skirt by lifting it over your head. Mortimer!

Eyes up!" My jaw began to ache from clenching it so tightly, and all I wanted to do was smack both my vampire friend and Dorie because I just knew I'd feel better if I hit someone at this point. I looked around, knowing we hadn't driven that far at all but didn't recognize the part of town we were in. And I wasn't paying all that much attention as I would have if I had driven, and Dorie told me when and where to turn.

"What kind of book do you have for us, Mortimer?"

"It's not I who owns this tome, Lily. But someone who informed me of its existence and needs you to retrieve it for him. You see...I left it behind in..."

"Mortimer Snodgrass! Don't you dare tell me I need to enter that highly unstable hellhole known as the Forbidden Library! Not if you want to remain on friendly terms with me!"

Mortimer shrugged sheepishly and held his hands out.

"I cannot believe this!"

"Believe it, Lily. We need this book. It has all the lore on what a sweet briar witch is plus some fascinating facts on sirens. You need this to battle the Council, not to mention the Order of Origin has been trying unsuccessfully to get their hands on it. We have to beat them to it before they discover the only copy has been in Morty's possession all this time!" Dorie emphatically informed me.

"Not in my possession, but I was aware of its existence back when I stayed in the Forbidden Library for a time. Had I known Lily would be this sweet briar witch, I might have tried to read some of the passages. But alas, I had no idea she was this entity. Nor do I think I possess the ability to touch this book," explained Mortimer. "Therefore, we must access the library and see what can be done."

"But I don't want to go back down there!"

"Yet you must. And I will aid you, Lily. And so will he," replied Mortimer.

"He? Who...oh! Grandpa Antonio. I didn't see you there."

"Ciao! Buon Giorno, Liliana. Pandorie, bella ragazza!"

Dorie giggled and simpered, and I smacked her. "Quit it."

"Ow."

"You too, old man. Flirting with a crossroads demon at your age. Give Dorie an inch and she'll steal your foolish old soul and sell it on the black market."

"Hey! I would not. Maybe."

I turned to address Mortimer who had inched away a few feet.

"Do you mean to tell me, not only do I have to go into the Forbidden Library—again—but this time I'm dragging a centenarian witch, a crossroads demon, and a vampire with me?"

"And me."

I whirled around at the sound of my Cousin Nora's voice, not believing what I was hearing. Then I stood there agog when I realized who—or what—she had with her.

"Wicked! Wait a second. Do you mean all this time, my cat has been hanging out with...with...you?"

Nora nodded, and I growled then stomped my foot.

"No way. I'm done. You may have helped me out over the holidays, Nora. But I am still trying to figure out if I should trust you completely or if you are up to something."

Nora had held out an olive branch of sorts over the Christmas holiday, claiming she wanted to let bygones be bygones and hoped to repair the damage she'd caused with her parents. The one thing to solidify her conviction and crack open the seal of mistrust I've been carrying with me, was her gift to Lorcan and me. Nora, unbeknownst to me, is now in charge of the magical banns book which records all the upcoming marriages. She graciously handed it over to Lorcan after sneaking it out of the Council building so we could write down the date of our wedding and sign our names. This was monumental, because once we signed on the dotted line, the magic sealed that date and nothing the Witch Council could do or say other than tossing me in a deep, dark dungeon somewhere could stop the wedding.

It was our little caveat to be revealed when and if the Council noticed—which they would, eventually.

So right now, I was sort of in Nora's debt. But I still couldn't bring myself to trust her completely, even after she set Wicked down so my ungrateful cat could run over to me.

"So, what's the story with her?"

"I've recently decided I don't like being played by Clarkson."

I raised my eyebrow but didn't comment further. Nora sighed and continued.

"Seeing as it's obvious to everyone except your fiancé that she is a snake whose sole purpose is to take Lorcan away from you..." Pandora's words came back to me, and all I could do was picture Lorcan staring at Tiffany in her shower. I felt sick to my stomach and almost missed what Nora said next. "I decided to keep pretending I like her. She's been doing subtle little things to put herself in Lorcan's path, and Wicked here, has been keeping tabs on her...with this." Nora held up a tiny cat collar that didn't look all that interesting until I noticed it had a wee little camera built into it.

"That's diabolical! But why keep this from me? Keep me worrying about Wicked?"

"I had no idea Wicked wasn't coming home at night. I swear it. I'd meet up with her every day outside June's shop, and she'd head over with me to "visit" Tiffany. She and I always have breakfast together before she goes off to work. Wicked and I would tail Tiffany without her knowing it, and your cat made sure to follow her and see what she's been getting into. Most of the time, we pulled away if she went on duty...but on two occasions, this past Saturday and Sunday,

Tiffany did not go to work, and Wicked continued tailing her. I reviewed the video feed and I think you'll find it interesting...you and Sheriff Buford. It seems Tiffany met up with that homeless man who died right before he showed up in your yard...if the time is right, that is. But I think it is. And she looked like she was threatening him."

Whoa.

"But what about Edith's family? You've been tight with them ever since she died."

"There are some weird things going on over there, and when I questioned Stella Langsford, I was told to mind my business. I don't think she really ever cared much for me. And now, well, I've seen some strange beings wandering around the woods behind their estate but every time I wanted to mention them to someone, my mind became fuzzy. Something evil is there. Thankfully, Dorie caught me at the café one day last week when I was confused and managed to pick up my thoughts. Once she did, everything became clear again."

"Thees all nice ma we go now. Pronto!"

Grandpa Antonio had been fidgeting but remained quiet listening to Nora and I go back and forth. I guess he was over waiting for us to stop chatting. I filed away what she'd said so she could discuss this further with Pandora and me. Turning to Mortimer, I continued my protestations.

"I really don't want to go back down in that scary dungeon."

"Library," interjected Mortimer.

"Same thing. I don't want to go down there again!"

"Lucky for you the Witch Council rebuilt it and moved its location. Jerry is positively apoplectic over it," continued Mortimer.

"Hey! Wait a minute. Isn't this the old Dairy Queen

behind the police station and the square? But...wow! Look at it down here! When did this happen?"

The decrepit area down the hill from the square, long abandoned, had a renaissance of sorts and many of the abandoned buildings had been spruced up—and moved up. Literally. The area used to flood regularly, which is why it was discarded in the first place, but it looked like the ground had been raised, dirt and vegetation brought in, and new roads paved. It was easily ten feet higher than it was the last time we were here...and looked like an extension of our shopping hub. How they managed to raise the buildings along with the land was a mystery until I realized magic had to have been employed.

"Whoa! There are even stairs leading up to the square! When did this happen?"

"Lily! Really! Before you got tossed off the board of Elders, you were one of those who signed the decree allowing for the beautification of empty lots and such. Have you forgotten?" Nora harrumphed, and I ducked my head in embarrassment.

"Um...maybe?"

Hey, I've had my hands full as of late!

"Anyway," Mortimer continued, barely concealing his long-suffering sigh, "we are using a diversion of sorts because things have changed as far as the Forbidden Library goes. It is now a section in this new arcane library for witches and other paranormals—the connection to Sweet Briar's library is gone. The last thing anyone needs is a stray human finding their way in."

Indeed. Oh, wait a minute!

"Please don't tell me we need to walk backward again. Grandpa Antonio will need to be carried or we'll be here all day! And what defensive mechanisms are set up to protect the closed section? I am not about to have my hand sliced open again!" I began looking around furtively to see if Adriana was lurking about.

Memories of the time she'd sliced my hand open and ran it across the protruding tongue of a door demon guardian had me balling my hands into fists and shaking my head. I wasn't being contrary...I just didn't like pain and pervy demons—the exception of course being Dorie, for the most part anyway, because she was most definitely pervy.

"No need to stress, Lily. This will be a rather...uh...pleasant experience if everything works out the way I've planned it. We are going to walk in, cause a mild distraction, have you run to the room to retrieve the book...take a peek inside to find the information on sweet briar witches, then sneak back out. Easy as pie. Shall we?"

Planned it? Sneak? Pie? How come I have a feeling things were about to go from mildly interesting to all-out war in about thirty seconds?

Mortimer and everyone present promptly turned around and began walking backward carefully toward the entrance. Again? Didn't I just say this would be an issue with my great-grandfather? Sighing, I watched as they made their way to the front door of the abandoned Dairy Queen, then I glanced back at my Jeep and stifled a scream.

Grandpa Antonio materialized directly in front of me.

Groaning inwardly, I acknowledged to myself that it would definitely take some doing to get him inside.

7

"This is bizarre."

"What is bizarre?" Mortimer—hand firmly grasping Antonio's collar—had just righted the centenarian and unbuttoned his long, black coat but paused to peer at me.

"This still looks like an abandoned Dairy Queen. The tables are all askew, but the kitchen area is intact. Where is the library?"

"This area still has to be converted back into a Dairy Queen in the unfortunate instance some human tourists might wander to this area whilst visiting your town and want a meal. The doors to the library will be housed up the hallway to our right and can only be accessed if you possess magic. Through those doors, right over there."

Mortimer jutted his chin out, using it to point at two very familiar looking doors—the very ones that led to the grand area of my Fairy Godfather Jerry's domain when he guarded the Forbidden Library. It was a room straight out of a Monty Python movie. The doors were green, padded, and looked like the ones you'd see in a high-end restaurant where the waiters would go in and out—complete with tiny windows. The only difference was the addition of the nasty demon guardian I mentioned. He was centered on one of the doors and was currently ogling me with a wicked glint in his eyes.

Speaking of Wicked, she'd puffed up and growled but stood her ground, tail swishing.

"I knew it! There is no way every single person who comes in here has to give a blood oath or whatever the heck it is I was forced to give the last time I saw this dude! I'm not going to freely give anyone present my hand!"

"That's why I'm here."

Quick as a whip, Adriana materialized out of thin air it seemed, and grabbed my wrist. The next few minutes had her attempting to drag me over to the door—she was 98 pounds soaking wet—and me easily setting my heels and not budging despite her best efforts. Grandpa Antonio beamed at our antics and clapped, although I wasn't sure if he was cheering his wife on or giving me support.

"I. Will. Not. Do. It. Old. Woman. Not!" Yes, I was speaking in all initial capitals, and no, I didn't think this was a bit dramatic.

"If you'd just let me...ow!"

"No."

"You are being a stubborn fool..."

"Yep!"

"Liliana! Stop this right now and let me explain!"

Sure, because I'm an idiot.

"Nope! I will not. I don't care how much you need this book, I... oof!"

That weasel! That nasty, two-faced, mentally unstable rat! She might look small and scrawny, but she certainly packed a wallop.

"You bit me! She *bit* me!" Holding my hand up to show the rest of the group, I remained transfixed by the tiny teeth marks now perfectly formed on the fleshy part of my hand between my thumb and pointer finger. "What is wrong with you? Now I'm going to need a rabies shot!"

"If you'd shut it and listen for a minute instead of acting like a spoiled brat, I'd explain," grumped Adriana. "You don't need to give a blood tribute to the demon door. He just needs to do an oratory assessment before you are allowed entry. We did not change the entrance requirements prior to you being removed from the Elders, so we need *your* hand to gain entry since you took over the position that was supposed to be held by Charles. Once we have time, I can have it switched to Charlie...or even myself until we get this straightened out and you back where you belong on the Elder Council. However, right now it is *your* hand I need."

"I'm confused. Oratory what?"

"Sniff, Lily. The demon guardian needs to sniff your wrist," said Pandora with a little snicker.

Oh. Well, that wasn't so bad then. Why did no one mention this prior to me making a fool of myself? Sometimes I think they do this just to watch me melt down and have something to discuss later around the dinner table.

"No cuts? No blood?"

"None."

Pulling my hand free from Adriana's death grip, I squared my shoulders and walked over to the grinning, malevolent face of the waiting demon.

"Ah! Lily Sweet, we meet again."

"Yes, well...you can just curb your enthusiasm. Sniff me, and let's get this over with."

The demon had the audacity to give me another once-over and an eyebrow wiggle. He'd done this the last time we met, leaving me with barely enough dignity to walk into the lower levels of the Forbidden Library, all the while feeling the need to shower. Now here he is again, ogling me like I'm a tasty morsel to fill his pervy needs. Just gross! Taking in a huge whiff, he slowly let it back out again with a grin and a comment. "Mmm...nice. I do love sniffing a good-looking witch first thing in the morning."

I'm sure my face looked like I'd just puked.

"OK, let's head in there. Now remember, we need to make sure the distraction is in full swing before we grab that book."

"Why can't we just ask Jerry for it or check it out again?" I asked.

"Because it is even more forbidden than usual. I even tried reasoning with Susanne Washington, but without a full tribunal of voting Elders, no one is going anywhere near the thing," replied Adriana with a frown. "And few can go up to it. We're hoping you'll be able to take it once we cause a mild disturbance. You will know which door to go through because it's the only other door once we enter from this side."

"Fine, let's get this over with." I made to push open the demon door but stopped short when he spoke once more.

"Not so fast. Entry is denied."

The room quieted as the demon's voice registered.

"What does that mean?" barked Adriana.

"I think it means we aren't allowed inside," said Dorie helpfully.

Adriana's scowl just deepened.

"Precisely that. I cannot allow you entry."

"And why is that? You sniffed Liliana. Let us in!"

The demon cut his eyes to Adriana and returned her perturbed glance with one of his own—only the frown on his face was something which would easily keep children up night...not to mention a few adults as well.

"Because she did not pass muster."

I was suddenly overcome with the urge to sniff my armpits, trying to recall the last time I showered, then shook my head.

"I do not smell!" My voice might have squeaked a bit. In my defense, my nerves were shot, and I still had visions of the horrors I'd witnessed the last time I was in the Forbidden Library. Nothing ever went right when in there...new location or not. Now my body odor was coming into question, and I for one, felt highly insulted.

"I did not state you had a repugnant odor—for a human witch, anyway. I said your smell did not pass muster."

"What the heck does that mean?" cried Adriana. Antonio slowly made his way over to Adriana and rested a hand on her shoulder for support.

"It means she does not smell like Lily Sweet should smell, therefore I cannot allow her—or you, as her companions —entry."

How do you like that? I am failing at my own body scent along with my witchy abilities. This has got to be some kind of joke...or maybe Fate was trying to tell me something. I certainly felt like Fate might be banging me over the head to get my attention. I just didn't know what the message they wanted to impart could be. It still didn't make sense...this demon had tasted my blood.

"But you know me. We've met already! It worked last time, and I haven't changed or anything. I'm still me! I don't understand how you can refuse us entry."

"Because your smell is not the smell of Lily Sweet. It's simple, really."

I heard subtle sniffing sounds coming from behind me and whirled to find Pandora standing way too close for comfort—especially since she was bent in half and sniffing close to areas I'd rather she not.

"What are you doing? Get away from me, Dorie!"

"It smells like Lily. In a way. I mean...I am picking up some kind of subtle differences, but nothing that would alarm me. It looks like her too."

It? Suddenly I'm an it?!

"OK. That's it. Get your nose away from me, Pandora. I'm done here. And I am *not* an it. I'm Lily Sweet. If this demon is too stupid to realize this then..."

"We could use blood, I guess," mused Adriana, rubbing her chin and giving me the once-over.

"Are you kidding me? I've already...hey!"

A shift in bodies had everyone present moving slightly in my direction, eyes intent and locked on mine, and I suddenly felt like a cornered animal—and reacted as such.

"Oh, no you don't!"

I took off running toward the abandoned kitchen, pushing Dorie out of my way in my rush to escape, which caused her to go down and take everyone with her. I gave a little cheer and dove behind the counter, scrambling to find something to keep a vampire, a demon, and three witches at bay—although on further inspection, Nora hadn't moved a muscle and was watching the hullabaloo with Wicked, who seemed bored by it all. The first thing I found was a soup ladle which had me trying to figure out what Dairy Queen ever served that required one and came up empty.

Thrusting the implement out in front of me, I pointed it every which way as I confronted my enemies, once friends and family, and uttered my warning in my most lethal-sounding voice.

"Don't come any closer or I will use this!" I shouted. OK, it was more like a shrill cry you'd hear from a scaredy-pants sissy out on the playground somewhere, but I did *try* to sound dangerous. I can't help it if I whimpered a little.

"Be reasonable, Liliana. One second of pain and..."

"Nothing! Because you aren't getting any blood from me!"

I made to run in the opposite direction when Mortimer loomed up on my left. Screaming, I forcefully threw the ladle which bonked his head and landed across the room. I felt my magic rising up, and knew I dare not use it on those I loved, even if they were trying to gut me.

"Everyone needs to stay back! Get away! Do not follow me!"

I hopped on the counter, preparing to let loose another shriek when I noticed everyone's bemused look...almost like they were confounded and befuddled but not in any particular harm. More like they were...

"Charmed? Are you guys OK?"

"Oh, now this is interesting," said Mortimer, who was repeatedly shaking his head as if to clear it.

"What happened to them? Look! Even Wicked seems fuzzy."

"I do believe you used your full siren voice for the first time, Lily Sweet. You've cast a spell...and on Adriana and Antonio too. My, my! You *are* a strong one."

"But...I didn't mean to hurt them!"

"You haven't harmed anyone, Lily. They should snap out of it shortly. You aren't in full command or know how to control it, but I am impressed, nonetheless. Most paranormals are unaware of this, but sirens are more akin to vampires than any other being. Certainly more so than mermaids with whom they tend to be associated. Yet sirens are *not* mermaids," explained Mortimer.

Huh. Now that I think about it, when I first heard about Tarni and it was explained to me what she was, I assumed mermaid. I have no idea what a siren is then...and that worried me.

"Are my eyes black, Mortimer?"

"Indeed."

Sigh.

"My fangs didn't punch out."

"That's because you chose siren over vampire," he stated.

"I don't think I did much choosing. I think it just happens. Oh, Mortimer! I really am a menace to society."

And look at that. In all the craziness, I managed to cut my wrist. Not deeply, but enough that it drew some blood. I held it up, cocking my eyebrow at Mortimer who smiled slightly and marched over to the demon door.

"Here. Lick it already."

Chuckling evilly, the demon did just that, and the door popped open.

I didn't even wait for Morty to round up the dazed and confused. Instead, I waltzed into the library like I owned the place and that was the biggest mistake I've ever made to date.

Why, oh, why didn't I just stay home?

8

"Lily Sweet...you cannot be here."

"Lily Sweet! No, no, no. You must leave immediately!"

"Stop right there! You are not allowed entry! Call the authorities! Call the authorities!"

I'd like to say I met a wall of Elders who I knew were against me and my family and they just happened to be in the new library at the same time we chose to storm in and steal a book. But no. I'd never had the pleasure—or in this case, pain —of meeting the three odd characters who accosted me the minute they spied me entering the room.

And I do mean accost. Two were hurling paper clips in my direction while the third held up a stapler with the intent—I suspect—to use the machine to tack the little u-shaped implements to my forehead.

Two were women, I assume paranormals of some sort. One was a man...I think. It was difficult to tell really, because all three wore the most outlandish garments I'd ever seen that I knew didn't come out of a catalog or store. Certainly not in these parts. The fabric was shimmery, the colors muted and several different shades...almost like a dull, subdued rainbow, all washed-out and bland. They were wrapped not unlike mummies, with only their faces showing. Seriously...from their feet on up they were wrapped thusly, even their hands didn't escape the cloth. The only thing that distinguished male from female was the scant amount of makeup on the two women and the obvious differences in chest depth. Although, if I had to swear on it, the third could have been a non-makeup wearing female with a lack of a protruding bosom. Some chicks were flat-chested, after all.

Their voices sounded similar, which freaked me out, and they glided when they walked.

"I'm sorry, but I have every right to be here. I do believe my family partially funded this library."

"Oh, no, no no! You mustn't come in. You are not welcome here, Lily Sweet."

"Forbidden!"

"Yes...forbidden!"

"Banned, dare I say!"

I kept dodging the frontal assault, barely controlling my sudden urge to zap these modern mummies to the next county. Especially when one overly enthusiastic toss had a small box of tissues conking me in the head.

"Quit it! I've been banned from the library? What reason does anyone have to ban me from a library?" I asked.

"You are a menace!"

"A book thief!"

"A renegade witch of ill repute."

Ill repute? Seriously?

"You can just go use the human library and burn that down. Leave this one alone, Lily Sweet."

Burn it down? I am pretty sure I've never met these imbeciles, and yet they are flinging accusations at me of arson and treachery. I for one, am insulted.

"Now, now! People! Step aside and let Lily be. Go back to

your duties this instant!" Jerry, my Fairy Godfather—just go with me on this—materialized behind the trio and shooed them away, although their reluctance was apparent. I was astounded at how quickly they backed down, bowing and scraping at Jerry, which gave me the impression not only was he the head honcho around here, but he also ruled with an iron fist.

"I'm so sorry, darling. My staff is a tad on the passionate side when it comes to protecting this new library. One suggestion from the Witch Council, and they go all gestapo on me."

While I was relieved to see a friendly face, it still rankled how maltreated I was in this town, and I had hurt feelings all around. This was probably one reason I remained aloof and stilted despite my love for my godfather.

"I'm sure they're plotting my death even now or have a nice cozy prison cell with my name on it. It seems everyone is against me."

"Oh, pudding! I hate that you are so upset. It makes your forehead pucker which ages you something horrible."

Gee, thanks.

"But hey! Listen...you are here now. We can have a nice little visit, then you can slip out of here fairly unnoticed since we are a bit slow today."

Whoa. Even Jerry wants nothing to do with me. He must have seen how his words affected my confidence. I was crestfallen and dejected. Nothing anyone could say at this moment could change my demeanor.

"Lily Sweet! Fancy seeing you here as I was just speaking to Sheriff Buford about you."

I looked up to find Dr. Clarkston, not to be confused with Clarkson, our new medical examiner, standing beside me near the front desk, with an armful of books ready to be checked out. "You do seem to have bad luck follow you around, young lady."

"Yep. That's me. I'm a real Debbie Downer."

"Now, I wouldn't say that. I wonder, did you hear the news? About Heathcliff Fitzwillow?"

I stared blankly at the nice doctor and blinked repeatedly. My total lack of response and vacant gaze must have indicated my lack of comprehension, for his face softened and he further explained. I wish he hadn't once I heard what he had to say.

"Heathcliff Fitzwillow was that vagrant who showed up at your house."

Ah, my crazy dead stalker. "The man who died. That was his name?"

"Well, see...that's the thing. He isn't dead. He showed up at the police station while I had been visiting, and about scared me and Sherriff Buford right out of our clothing! Especially since I came from the morgue to inform Glen that no bodies turned up as of yet."

"Hang on a minute! What? How could he be alive?"

"Whoever called the sheriff stating they were from the hospital, lied. The man is alive and well and only suffered some third degree burns on his hands. He had no idea who might have called in he was dead...but he did have something you might consider highly interesting to say to Glen."

"I can't imagine. What did he say?"

"He wanted to know if the 'intense lady' could be arrested for non-payment and veiled threats...and could he get his money some other way. When Glen asked him what he meant, Heathcliff went on to say a highly intimidating woman hired him to make you look bad and accuse you of witchcraft...which is ironic, if you ask me. I mean...you are a witch. What else should you be doing but witchy stuff?"

Indeed.

"Last I saw, the sheriff was heading out to have a little talk with Wilhelmina Dietrich. I wouldn't want to be in her shoes right about now."

Well, at least that was going in my favor. Maybe, in light of the Dietrichs and Langsfords scheming and plotting, the tide would turn. I mean, it had to have been one of them who paid this man to accuse me. Who else could it be? Maybe now folks in town would look more favorably at me and my plight. I'm being framed, and my good name sullied. I didn't mean to be a spaz magically. I really didn't! I'd worked very hard practicing my magic for well over a year now, and this aberration of mine wasn't because I lacked the ability. Something was mucking with me—and perhaps we were close to getting answers. If I could keep the wolves at bay long enough to do something about it—some research and fact-finding.

I bid the doctor a good day as he hustled out of the library with a spring to his step, whistling a little tune.

Turning back to Jerry, I wondered at the absence of my "team" of mischief makers. Where were they? Could they still be bemused?

"Jerry, I am looking for a book on sweet briar witches. Would you have something on that...maybe in the Forbidden Library, that I might possibly peek at?"

All the color drained from Jerry's face, which was saying a lot considering he had more makeup on than a drag queen on a Friday night before showtime.

"Oh, no. Listen dollface, you know I adore you...but I cannot let you near that book. No one is even supposed to know it exists. How did you find out about it? Wait. Adriana...and Antonio, of course. They purchased it close to 60 years ago now for the Forbidden section. How could I forget? Well, you can't go near it, toots."

"But, Jerry..."

"But, Jerry nothing. The last thing you or anyone else needs is to read it and see that stupid premonition."

Premonition? I felt my blood run cold at Jerry's words and knew, whatever was written in this book, whatever dire prediction came with it, involved me in some way because I'd already been named this sweet briar witch. Adriana's parents...yeah, I know—shocking to have great-great-grand-parents running around, looking like they were in their 70's and living it up in Florida—had informed everyone without a doubt I was a sweet briar witch. But what does it all mean? Nothing had ever gone further, and my family tried to keep it on the down-low.

Hey! Hang on a minute!

"Jerry! How did you find out? I mean...the town in general, the Elders. Who told everyone I was this sweet briar witch thingy?"

Jerry lowered his eyes and sighed, then met my eyes once more. "That's just it, Lil. You might *not* be the sweet briar witch. Right now, a massive manhunt—or witch hunt rather—is underway for Tarni Vanderzee. There are two possible sweet briar witches among us, you...or Tarni. This is no joke because the sweet briar witch is the bringer of doom—or so says this prognostication. Lily...if it's you, well, I don't know what will happen."

"Jerry...please. You know me. You know I had no idea growing up who or what I am. Please allow me to read the book. I won't take it anywhere...and I won't lie to you. My family is on the other side of that door, plotting to sneak in and remove the book from the Forbidden Library, but I am here asking, not sneaking around. Please let me read it. I will sit right beside you and never move from that spot until I'm finished. Pretty please?"

I could see Jerry pondering my words and wavering with every second that went by. Finally, he rose up to his full height, which...seeing as how he was a little person and sans his usual stiletto footwear, meant he was eye level to my belly-button, didn't mean much. But he snapped his fingers like an imperial leader summoning his serfs, and over scurried the three minions who waited expectantly for his orders.

"Filbert. Bring me the key for the lower section."

A gasp of sheer dread went through the trio, and they looked dubiously in my direction.

"But, sir. I must insist you reconsider. This...this...persona non grata cannot be allowed down there."

Jerry didn't move a muscle or blink, but the intensity of his stare deepened, and I could hear the audible gulp from all three of his underlings.

"Yes, sir."

Meekly, the one named Filbert slunk off toward an elabo-rate cabinet—all filigreed and ornately carved wood with a glorious patina that possessed multiple intricate locks—and proceeded through the long, laborious process of opening each one to procure said key. It didn't surprise me when Jerry palmed the item, holding the large key firmly in one hand, and I spotted a tiny devil head on one end instead of a skeleton as I assumed. Cute touch, that.

Jerry waltzed over to a huge wooden door with iron hinges and studs and inserted the key into the lock. With a loud "click," the door opened and cool air with the hint of something antediluvian assaulted my nostrils. It wasn't unpleasant...but it gave me the willies nonetheless because with that hint of age came something else...something malevolent.

"Come on, Lily. You might as well come along with me."

Suddenly, the overwhelming urge to run came over me, but I asked for this, so...onward.

I just hoped this would take a few minutes and no more. I mean, we were just retrieving one book...right?

9

Jerry and I had just reached the bottom step when my memory clicked, and I latched on to his arm like it was my lifeline to the surface and safety.

"Jerry! Sentinels! Do you have them here? What is guarding this level? Oh my gosh...please let's go back up before they arrive."

Jerry chuckled, his face glowing eerily with the low light hitting us from flaming wall sconces.

"Calm down, cookie puss. We don't have those nasty things here in this facility."

Oh, jeebers was I grateful. The last thing I wanted to deal with was...

"We have something far worse."

I stopped short, causing Jerry to stumble a little since I was still clutching his right hand.

"Oof! Lily! What's wrong? Why did you stop?"

"Worse? Like worse, worse? How can anything be worse than two Sentinels, oozing and gnashing horribly yellowed teeth in their multiple mouths?"

Jerry took a steadying breath before explaining, and I swear he'd just managed to not roll his eyes.

"We have pixies. Pandora gave me the suggestion. Apparently, she convinced a tribe of them to focus their energy on becoming guardians rather than making mischief on the outside and run the chance of terrorizing some human. So now, I have a crack team of pixies on guard duty. And let me tell you...they are legend."

Pixies?

"You mean...Chuck is down here with his friends?"

"Not Chuck. No. He is on a special mission with three or four of his buddies for Pandora...although she wouldn't let me in on what their mission entails. But it *is* his group I have here working for me...and I am sure Chuck will be along soon. Once he's completed whatever it is Pandora has asked of him."

I'm sure. Now I wondered what Dorie had done. Obviously, she is up to no good. How do I know this? Because I didn't know anything...not about her mysterious trip, not about her taking Chuck, et al along with her, not about her commandeering the pixies to turn from their less than stellar shenanigans to legitimate work...none of it. Therefore, I had a bad feeling about where all this would eventually lead.

"But Jerry...pixies? Scarier then Sentinels?"

"You have no idea."

Doubting the verity of his warning, I marched along the corridor until we came to one last door. Upon entry to the next room, I couldn't help but notice the vast difference this library was from the old one. This seemed downright pleasant. Like something out of Beauty and the Beast, all mahogany shelves and an iron ladder and tall windows with... snow? Wait...windows? Weren't we underground at this point?

"Neat, huh?"

"Gah!"

Turning quickly, I discovered the woman of the hour standing behind us.

"Dorie! What have you been up to woman? Pixies? This? And where is Chuck?"

"Don't worry about Chuck. I owed him one, and I always follow through on those...especially with pixies."

I shifted my chin, regarding both Jerry and Dorie who'd given each other knowing looks.

"And where is everyone else?"

"Stuck upstairs waiting for your magic to wear off. It didn't get Mortimer but for a few seconds...me a few after that. Everyone else remained bemused and silly for quite some time and are still a bit wonky. You have some strong siren magic coursing through those veins of yours, Lily," stated Dorie. "But I knew that."

Great. Just what I needed in light of the Witch Council and their analysis of my personality and level of danger.

"Well, we're down here and I don't see any scary, old pixies to.... argh!"

I spoke too soon. Transforming in front of us next to one of the bookshelves was the most terrifying creatures I'd ever seen to date. Like seriously, nothing else could ever come close to the horror that stood before me, and I tried in vain to recall what a teeny-tiny pixie looked like—because this twelve-foot beast was definitely not one!

"What is that?!"

Jerry smiled and began tugging me toward the hideous visage. "That is Justine. Or are you Helena? I can never tell when you come out in full glory."

"Creep flurb pfft."

"Ah, Justine it is. Hello, my dear."

Are you kidding me? It speaks? Or whatever the heck it just did? And Justine?

"Groo uck uck thlurb sheez!"

"I know. But this is a special occasion, and my goddaughter, Lily, needs to see one of our tomes."

"Leevthsssslee! Neex! Neex!"

I do believe the terrible creature just denied Jerry's request. Either that or something pinched it because it jumped and swelled to epic proportions and frowned at me. And here I was being as mild and pleasant as I could manage in light of standing before what could only be described as liquid snot. Jerry was right—this was far more disturbing than the Sentinels.

"Foop!"

It pointed its arm—OK, it oozed in my direction, but really, I'm trying to be descriptive here—and growled. That's when I noticed a second one come rushing in my direction, and I shoved Pandora in front of me as a shield.

What? I'm not stupid!

"Foop!"

"Eeej, foop! Foop!"

The first glop of goo came too close for comfort, and I may or may not have whimpered a little.

"Foop you, moron. Get out of the way before I make you shrink to the size of a firefly and stick you in a jar for my desk," cried Dorie.

Desk? She doesn't even have a house. But I wasn't about to correct her. Not while she was standing up to these repulsive beasts.

"Foop!" The first pixie backed off after one last utterance, then shriveled down to a tiny perfect little purple person, complete with fairy wings, and sulked. She looked like a tiny reject from the Tinkerbell movies.

I whirled around and watched as the other one—Helena—did the same, but she threw Pandora a nasty look and blew a raspberry. This one was green and could almost pass as Tink if it wasn't for the long, pointy teeth she bared at me before hissing and stomping her tiny foot.

Nice.

"Here, Lily. Come sit at this table, and I will retrieve the book in question. I must warn you though...touch it not. Allow either myself or Dorie to do the honors. I fear the book will react to such a strong dark witch and, well...I don't know what will transpire if you do."

"Got it. Keep my hands to myself. Dorie turns the pages."

Jerry nodded in satisfaction at my words, then went in search of the book we needed.

Just then, Adriana and the rest of my group came lumbering into the room...and the atmosphere went from bad to worse.

"Nice job back there, Squirt. Next time remind me to bind your mouth so you don't inadvertently go off and bewitch the lot of us."

"Who said it was inadvertent?" I tossed back.

Adriana pointed her long, boney finger at me, and I blanched a little but held my ground. Adriana didn't scare me. Much. Not really.

"Don't try me, Squirt. You won't like the results. I don't play fair."

"Tell me about it—or rather, tell me about Jared. When did you find yourself a willing shifter?"

"Never you mind about him. We have more pressing matters," replied Adriana.

"Fine. But I want to know all about him when we have a moment to discuss everything."

Wicked came trotting over to the table and hopped up, then sat directly in front of me, staring with enigmatic eyes. It looked like she was trying to convey a message, but I was still rather upset with her for going off without a word. Suddenly, her green eyes widened, and she went into a crouch and began to wiggle her butt. When I gazed across the room to see what caught her attention, I was horrified to find her about to spring up and pounce on Justine. The little pixie didn't see the jaws of doom about to take her out!

"Wicked, no!"

But my admonishment came too late. Wicked launched into the air, arms outstretched and claws out. I knew the little pixie wouldn't stand a chance and watched in horrified fascination. It all seemed to be happening in slow motion, and I briefly wondered if another witch with better control of their magic would step in and save the little fairy.

But it wasn't Justine who needed saving.

Just as Wicked reached the tiny figure, it transformed into a hideous monster with a large gaping maw that opened, showing glittering sharp teeth and a lolling purple tongue...and it swallowed my cat entirely.

"Wicked! Oh my gosh, no! Someone save her!"

I flexed my fingers preparing to blast whatever the heck the monster was into oblivion when it began to cough and hack and spit my tiny furball of fury back out into the room with one last shuddering cough. Then it turned back into Justine and flew onto a high shelf where it continued to sputter and hack, throwing dark looks all around.

"Oh my! Justine! You know better than to tease cats! Especially one as smart as Wicked."

Jerry retuned to the room just in time to witness my cat being upchucked onto the floor and Justine's flight. I turned to confront him but stopped short when I noticed that large tome in his hands. Not only was it quivering, it was all Jerry could do to hold it steady, and I believed it would spring from his hands, grow legs, and run off if it could. A sentient book? How astounding! But it didn't stop me from scolding my Fairy Godfather.

"How could you keep such dangerous things around ready

to eat someone...or something? Wicked could have been killed by that...that..."

"Oh, Justine was only messing with Wicked. She wouldn't have eaten her. If that were the case she would have morphed into a hellhound."

Seeing as I had experience with hellhounds, I gave the little fairy a wary look and leaned toward Jerry. "Are they shifters? The pixies? What is going on here?"

"They can transform themselves into temporary beings as long as they study the structure of whatever they are about to transform into. They prefer scary beings so as to become something no one in their right mind would want to attack. It makes them handy at guard duty...because who would want to take on a troll...or a dragon for that matter."

"Yes. I could see...wait, what?"

"OK...about this book. What do you know of it, Jerry?" This was from Adriana, and I was concerned at how fast she brushed away the dragon comment. Dragons? Really?

"I know it is ancient and dangerous. I'm not at all happy you have chosen to disturb it—there is a reason it's in the Forbidden Library after all, Adriana. When you bequeathed it to the library all those years ago, I knew you had no idea what you possessed. This book is a chancy maneuver to discover something no one knows much about...even for you. If something goes wrong, well...I'm not sure what will happen."

"Nothing will happen. I am here, after all. And no book is going to keep me from helping my great-granddaughter."

Well, that was sweet in a way, but I didn't want to be the reason all hell broke loose, and the world came to an end.

"Perhaps a lesson in how to approach this might be prudent," suggested Mortimer, looking askance at the quivering book.

"But that's just it. No one alive, to my knowledge, knows

exactly how to open it nor read it if they should. Perhaps your parents, Adriana, may have some knowledge...but even the oldest vampires in the area are at a loss when it comes to the Black Grimoire."

"That's what it's called?" I asked.

"Indeed. And it's legendary. How we wound up with it here in Sweet Briar has more to do with the name of the town and the founders...and is itself a controversial subject, and your great-grandparents knack for taking things they should best leave alone. But that's another story for another time. Adriana knows of what I am speaking. It was her kin who stole it from the Great Library in Rome and brought it to their mansion well over two hundred years ago now."

All eyes turned to Adriana, who shrugged.

"So what? My family is already infamous. My father Luigi offered to return it when he'd discovered the treachery, but no one in Rome wanted it back nor knew how to transport it from our family vineyard back to the Bibliotheca. Touching this book is perilous and could be deadly."

"And yet you managed to take it out of Italy all the way to Sweet Briar. And now wanted me to sneak in here and steal it," I grumbled.

"Hey, I figured you had a better chance of it than the rest of us, oh mighty dark witch. Plus...you are the sweet briar witch, so it figures you should be the one to try," sniffed Adriana.

"But you two have already touched it. You brought it here years ago!" I cried.

"When we had a certain spell cast on the tome to render it harmless for a certain period of time. That spell is long gone, and the book is back to being a danger."

"I don't understand. Jerry is holding it...he brought it in from the back room. Why is he able to do this?" asked Nora.

She stepped away from the table once Jerry placed the book on it and was hugging the back wall nearest the exit door.

"I have my own spells of protection for being the librarian in charge that aids me in my duties, dusting the books, shelving them, checking them out. But to actually open the book? To use the magic inside? No. I don't have the power. It knows...this book. It's aware that I am its keeper, but it would turn on me in an instant if it thought I'd try to pry open its secrets. Heck, it might mean the end of us all, should Lily make an error."

How do you like this load of malarky? Getting to be the most powerful dark witch in decades not only came with a set of problems that might make me reconsider the benefits, but now it looks like I'm expected to put out all these fires even if it means the destruction of anyone and everything if I make the slightest mistake. No pressure. Not at all.

Yeah, right.

"You have got to be kidding me! Do you people not get it yet that I'm over all of this? I'm done. Finished. Caput. I'm turning in my witch card as of this very moment and refuse to be part of anything magical ever again."

I gazed at everyone with my most severe face and made to move toward the door when I heard something that stopped me cold and made my skin crawl.

"Is that...is the book chuckling?"

"Indeed, I am, Lily Sweet. Come closer and let me have a look at you, precious."

Oh well, this is a fine how-do-you-do.

10

"How is it that you know me? A book, aware of someone that for sure has never met you, opened you, or read one single page of you...it's astounding!"

"I know many things. I know when I am near someone worthy to open my cover and read my pages. Come, sit down, and see what I have hidden in my chapters."

While this intriguing discourse was happening, everyone else in the room fell silent and stepped back, giving me space, yet leaving me feeling exposed. It struck me again how weird all these magical happenstances continued to be for me and how those here grew up with such activity. They hardly batted an eye when the book began to speak. Me? Not so much. My stomach was doing somersaults, and I felt queasy.

"You won't bite...right?"

A deep chuckle reverberated around the room, but the book chose not to respond. OK, so I think he's expecting our upcoming transaction as one that needs to be based on trust. Unfortunately, it was me who'd get a finger taken off should he decide to misbehave. Menacing didn't come close to describing the vision in front of me. All black, gloss, sharp, angular, wicked, and malevolent...the book certainly had hubris.

"I guess as the sweet briar witch, I'm worthy."

"Are you now? Are you sure? Read my passages to find out, Lily Sweet," he replied.

I say 'he,' because the voice sounded masculine, deep, and ancient. I'd never heard anything remotely female sound like that...but you never knew. I'm sure Maureen Kennedy sounded like a water buffalo in the mornings—but I digress.

Taking a deep breath and mumbling a soft, "here goes nothing," to myself, I reached out, placed my hands on either side of the book to pull it close, and opened the clasp, turning to the first page. Then frowned.

"I can't read this. I don't know the language in which it's written, nor do I recognize it."

"Keep turning my pages until you find the passage you are able to understand, Lily Sweet, those words are not for you...or anyone else in this room." This, the book stated a bit louder, and I could feel the air stir behind me, making me realize someone had tried to take a peek—probably Adriana, who quickly retreated.

Ha. That put me in a better place in my mind!

I turned the pages, careful not to damage the paper, which seemed somehow fragile despite the book appearing to be in pristine condition. The paper felt off, like something I'd never touched before in my life, and I wondered if it was held together by magic.

Well, duh, Lily...it's a magical book!

Suddenly, I came to a passage that jumped out at me, not only because I could read it, but it came on a page that had simple sketches of two women as well. Two women that looked suspiciously like me and Tarni Vanderzee. But how could this be? I've never met this book nor sat for any such drawing! This was astounding. Magic again...what else could it be?

"I found something! May I read it aloud?" I asked the book.

"By all means," it replied.

I cleared my throat and began to read.

Two shall come, but at different times. One will set in motion things which left unchecked could alter the paranormal world and bring ruin. The other will strive to fix these actions but nothing can stop the destruction.

Many shall consider these events the work of evil...but in time all shall be revealed and what was written in the stars will set the tide for the future. The paranormal world will be rocked to its foundations—chaos will reign—what will become of it when the dust clears? Only the Sweet Briar Witch can lead them through this by her tenacity and stubborn resolve. Yet which one is it? How about both...two equal sides of one whole.

Yet their paths are different.

As one fades, the other rises.

As one escapes her dark destiny and finds unexpected yet unwanted freedom, the other takes on the role of trailblazer.

Both carry the same genes.

Both hold the darkness in hand.

Both shall be considered Sweet Briar Witch, do not let this distract.

Only one will use it wisely.

The other will use it impulsively...yet admirably.

Both are wrong, yet both are right.

They balance each other even as the scales tip and the world trembles.

All attempts to stop them will fail.

One has to feel overwhelming loss to give the other her wings.

Time will prove this action right.

Both are dangerous, yet necessary. Both must not be challenged.

To resist what will come is folly.

Don't judge a book by its cover...it will lead to madness.
Sweet Briar Witch = destruction and change.
Let she who will be prosecuted fly free in the face of this destruction.
Let she who would fight for justice drown in her sorrow. Let she who
would sacrifice all fall to depths impossible to return from... only to
return. Let she who would falter in uncertainly, fail—alone—then
rise to greatness, only to fail again, and again. Let she who would find
frustration at every turn become strong from adversity.
Destruction of long held tenets, a way of life.
Seeking the way shall bring strife.
Love lost. Love found. Never on their terms while on solid ground.
Love found on firm earth, yet broken in due course, will prevail with
force.
Which one shall triumph?
Both.
Yet none shall succeed in the way expected.
It is written in stone, unable to be broken. It shall come to pass.
The Sweet Briar Witch is among us.

Lovely. That made zero sense to me, and from the faces of everyone present, I'd say they were equally perplexed. Before the book could slam shut or the words fade or whatever crazy arcane thing might happen, I pulled out my phone and snapped a photo so I could go over the passage whenever I needed.

I stared at the drawings. It looked like Tarni, perched on a rock, holding an item in her hand which was extended toward me, while I was sitting on an opposite rock about to take the item offered. That's when knowledge of what I was staring at slammed into me.

The ring! The aquamarine ring Tarni gave me the last time we met. I recalled her words and played them through my head.

"I am going to meet my destiny. My fate awaits me, and I shall not return. Here. Take my parting gift to you and remember this: you are one of the strongest dark witches to ever walk this earth. Don't let anyone take that power away from you. Not hate, not love, not allegiance, or loyalty to a cause, not fear. Nothing. Nothing should make you give up the power coursing through your body. Embrace it, witch, and siren. Embrace it and be the powerful force you were born to be. Take this ring. Wear it always. Answer your inner siren's call and allow it to strengthen. Don't let that voice be silenced. Ever. Farewell, sweet Lily."

And what had I done? I tucked the ring away in my jewelry box and hadn't looked at or worn it since. What was wrong with me? Tarni gave me that and perhaps all this silly wonky magic could have been avoided had I just worn it. I knew one thing—I'd be putting it back on and nothing would get it off my right hand ever again. Dare I tell anyone in this room about it?

I wasn't sure, so I kept my mouth zipped...although Wicked was giving me that knowing look again, and I suspected she had been aware of this all along.

"But what does it mean...to be the Sweet Briar Witch?" I asked the book. "While the passage is cryptic, I can easily tell it explains nothing about what being one means!"

"The Sweet Briar Witch is destruction and renewal. Chaos and clarity. She who is born to take up this mantle shall be feared, yet revered, loved, yet hated. Are you the one, Lily Sweet? Only time will tell."

That's it? No further explanation? What if it's been Tarni all along and I'm an imposter?

"But what if I'm not?

"I cannot say. But I will tell you, the Sweet Briar Witch does not know what she is."

After saying those additionally cryptic words, the book

fell silent, and the magic seemed to dissipate. So did my resolve.

❧

"But what does it all mean? I don't understand any of it, and I wonder if the book is toying with us," grumbled Adriana over her plate of meatloaf and mashed potatoes. If Adriana was mystified, I was downright bamboozled.

We'd said goodbye to Mortimer, who graciously offered to drive Antonio home while Adriana, Pandora, and Nora joined me at Joe's Diner for lunch. Wicked remained by my side, but my nose was still out of joint, although I was secretly relieved she'd not run off to places unknown the minute we were on the outside of the library.

"All this time I thought you a fraud and a weak excuse for a dark witch...and here you are something out of legend," murmured Nora with a frown. "I mean, we've heard our entire lives that Sweet Briar was special because it was named not only for the rose bushes prominent in these parts, but for the legendary witch who would bear the name and bring chaotic change for the better...although some believe it means for the worst."

"And it just happens to be our Lily here," snickered Pandora, giving my head a little pat.

"Liliana, eat your food. It's growing cold," chided Adriana. "We don't have valid proof that Liliana is any such thing. It could very well be Tarni. But right now, my great-grand-daughter needs food in her stomach!"

How could I think about eating? I'm a monster! A bringer of doom and destruction or a path to change that means...what? Happiness? Joy? My luck it would mean the end of the world for all paranormal beings. No wonder the Order of Origin wanted me nullified!

I pushed a carrot around my bowl. I'd opted for the beef stew but couldn't bring myself to enjoy it, despite the enticing aroma assaulting my nostrils, begging me to dive in. I had a sour taste in my mouth, and I wanted to slink off to parts unknown and have a good cry.

"I can't. My stomach feels like it's full of lead. It has to be me...I'm the only one who grew up not knowing what I was!"

"Nonsense. You are overreacting. We need to figure out what that passage means and move on from there."

"But what if it means I destroy everything in the paranormal world? That's sort of the consensus here. Let's face it...I'm the walking menace. Obviously, I'm the bringer of destruction. And all that love stuff at the end? Lorcan and I are doomed, I'm telling you."

"Sounds like someone is having cold feet about her relationship. You should have thought of that before ruining someone's life by making promises you can't keep." I quickly looked up, expecting to have harsh words with Nora, only to realize she wasn't the one who had spoken. Turning in incredulity at the audacity of listening in to a private conversation had me locking gazes with none other than Tiffany Clarkson.

"May I help you?" I asked, giving her my coolest glare.

"You heard me. I think it's a shame what you're doing to someone as gentle and empathetic as Lorcan. He seems trapped in a relationship with someone who is dangerous, toxic, and up to no good. Imagine that kind man tied to a renegade witch. It will ruin his reputation in this town and beyond...already has, if the lack of work around his shop is any indication. It's like he made a deal with the devil and needs someone to save him," she said with a slight giggle.

That giggle came out more depraved than I'd ever heard from that wretch. What does this shrew know of anything to do with Lorcan and his mechanic shop? He made me promise not to tell a soul. How did Tiffany discover his secret? Unless? No. I refused to believe anything this woman was spewing, even as a niggling bit of doubt ate its way into my consciousness. After all...Lorcan must have said something to Tiffany if she knew. Why would Lorcan share his business woes with her?

"I think you need to back off. You know nothing about me...or my relationship with Lorcan. How could you?" I snapped.

"Oh, Lily...the devil is in the details, my dear," purred Tiffany, showing a flash of teeth.

"Move along, missy. Unless you want me up in your business," barked Adriana menacingly.

Wicked actually stood, arched her back, and hissed. Good girl!

"I'm going to let the fact that you just threatened an officer of the law pass," stated Tiffany in a loud voice one used on the hard of hearing. "Especially since I'm certain you missed your meds this morning, Ms. Dolce. It must be difficult being so old and such." Lowering her voice once more, Tiffany continued, "Y'all have a blessed day now. Not that I expect you to. Nora, I'm sad to see you forced to be among your repugnant kin. You might want to watch with whom you associate." Flicking her eyes to Dorie then back at me, I caught the evil glint buried deep in Tiffany's eyes before she pulled down the veil of impassivity.

"You know, Lily...a man like Lorcan won't put out all your fires forever. He is too good and kind and just to put up with your brand of chaos. A time is coming soon when Lorcan is going to walk away and be grateful he escaped. After all, good men don't suffer evil—even if it's wrapped up in a pretty package." And with that parting shot, the unpleasant officer took her leave.

"I'm going to wring that snake's neck and make shoes out

of her skin." Adriana tracked Tiffany's progress across the street as she made her way toward Lorcan's shop...and her apartment beyond.

I felt sick to my stomach and wanted to wallow in pity. All the fight seemed to have vanished out of me, and I felt beaten.

"What is wrong with you, Lily? I can understand feeling a tad dejected, but you didn't defend yourself or your relationship with Lorcan!" cried Nora. "I don't understand. What happened to your spunk?"

What happened indeed. Maybe it would be better if I just left town, left my witchy life behind, and started anew somewhere where I wasn't known. Perhaps Lorcan made a mistake and refused to admit it...trying to be kind and all.

"Meroow!"

Wicked padded across the table and jumped into my lap. She put her nose inches from mine forcing me to look into her glowing green orbs.

"What? Get off me you silly cat."

"Meowrroo?"

Sighing, I scratched behind her ears. "I don't speak cat, Wicked."

Put on your ring!

"What? Who said that?"

I glanced at my three dining companions, knowing it wasn't their voices I heard. Looking around the diner, I caught the eye of Sheila, our waitress and friend who came rushing over.

"What can I get you, Lily? A refill? You haven't touched much of your food." Looking down at my plate and frowning, Sheila gave me an uncertain smile.

"No. Nothing, Sheila. But I have a question. Do you have any radio stations playing? I mean...other than the music? Maybe a TV show on in the kitchen or something?"

"Um...no. Is everything OK, Lily?"

"No. I mean yes! Yes...I'm fine," I said lamely, wishing I could slide under the table.

Adriana had one eyebrow cocked and gave me a scathing look. "What's wrong? If misery had a photograph, it would be yours."

"Leave Lily alone. She's just frazzled after the last few days she's endured," said Dorie in my defense.

Nora remained quiet, but I noticed she was watching Wicked closely.

"It's nothing, Sheila. I just thought I heard voices."

"Voices?!" cried the woman, looking around like she expected something to pop up from behind the counter.

"Well, a voice. One voice. Look, it's nothing. I'm tired is all."

"Lily! Oh, you poor darling. Donald told me all about your ordeal, and now I find you here looking like a lost little lamb." Doreen Murphy, another friend, and the woman I'd briefly stayed with on my first days in Sweet Briar came bustling over to me and gave me a squeeze. "How are you, dear?"

"I've had better days, Doreen. How are you?"

"Oh! Fair to middling, what with the winter doldrums in full swing and me unable to work in my garden. These old bones are just waiting for spring to return. How's business been?"

"It's doing rather well. I haven't slowed down much since Christmas, and my orders are still coming in. Molly is a godsend and works my booth on the days we are open and the weather permits."

Stop yapping and go put that ring on!

"Gah!" I jumped straight up, knocking Wicked onto the seat in our booth and scrambled into the aisle away from our table. I didn't stop until my back hit the counter. "I need to go. I'm sorry. I... I'll see you later."

I didn't listen to the exclamations of alarm or questions being hurled at me. I just ran out of the diner as fast as I could...so fast, I didn't notice Wicked had slipped out to follow.

Despite my refusal to admit it to myself, I knew exactly where that voice was coming from...and had I seen Wicked trailing after me, I might have run screaming like a banshee into the hills. As it stood, I wanted to get home quickly and take another gander at that ring before anyone decided to follow me!

11

Sitting on the floor in my bedroom and staring at the box where I'd tossed the ring, I pondered my actions. As much as I respected Tarni, what made me discard the ring she gave me without much thought to the consequence? The minute it was brought to my attention once more, memories of that moment came flooding back, making me realize someone or something had caused another memory loss.

I was not new to such a phenomenon.

What was novel was my reluctance to run screaming for Adriana or another relative to have a shoulder to cry on. It became apparent that my memory had been altered and or messed with enough to keep me from wearing Tarni's gift. But the second that veil was stripped away, another unexpected and welcome result happened. The mopey, woebegone, hide-in-my-house, sulky, whiny, pathetic wretch that I'd been as of late had disappeared, only to be replaced by the woman I'd become in recent months. I once again felt like the dark witch I was born to be.

Who could have tampered with me unawares, causing the lesser me to take over?

I sensed a presence behind me and relaxed when I felt Wicked weave around by body and crawl into my lap.

"You knew. You've always known, haven't you? I'd slowly become—maybe not hostile to you—but definitely unappreciative of just how special a cat you are. I assume I heard your voice in my head?"

Wicked just gazed at me, rewarding me with one of her slow kitty blinks.

"Well, I'm back and I'm pissed. Somehow, all along, I was aware I'd been a whiny pain in the butt. But I couldn't pull myself out of the funk. That's stops today."

"Merow!" said Wicked, then reached out and pawed the aquamarine ring as if to say, "Put it on already, woman!"

I picked up the beautiful piece of jewelry and felt the magic coursing through it. My tie to Tarni Vanderzee was not only one of blood, but of friendship. She'd allowed me to swim to the bottom of Nichol's Pond, giving me oxygen. She gave me one of her tears. I don't know the entire sordid tale of her life, nor did I care at this point, I just knew I'd fight for her without question—and take up the mantle of Sweet Briar Witch if that was my only option, because I owed her.

Slipping the ring on my finger, the power electrified my system, weaving its way into me like blood flow until I tingled with the possibilities of what I might achieve. Me. Lily Sweet. The town menace.

"Menace no more, that is. I don't know what happened, but I am about to find out who did this to me and give them one heck of a thrashing."

"That sounds more like my bestie."

"Dorie, um...what are you doing?" I became mildly alarmed when the sniffing began in earnest again as I found the crossroad demon behind me.

"All better. Nothing, Lil. I was just checking, and it seems you are back to smelling like you should. I knew something was up...especially after you ran off and left your precious Jeep parked at the diner. I drove it home, by the way, and didn't hit a thing. Now...it couldn't be the fact that you haven't been wearing that ring...or is it?" she asked.

"No. Maybe. I'm not sure. But someone—yet again—messed with my memory, and obviously did something to change *me* as well. How about you tell me why you had that bow on you and what your plans are to set things straight around here? I'm feeling rather punchy... if you know what I mean."

Pandora beamed at me, then let out a throaty chuckle. "Oh, Lily. Sweet Briar is not going to know what hit it once we're done. You still have that wicked dagger Adelaide gave you?"

"I do."

"Then suit up, kiddo. You and I are going on a little hunting expedition."

"I'm down with that... but the cat goes with us!"

"Rowrr!" said Wicked.

I couldn't agree more.

"So, where are we heading?" I asked as I put on my seatbelt and glanced at Dorie.

"We are going to the Dietrich compound to do a little snooping."

I steadied myself and liked that I didn't fly off the handle with worry. It made me aware of how much I'd changed in a few short months...and it ticked me off that I'd become such a wimp.

"I assume you have a plan or know of a way inside without getting caught?"

"Not really. But we have a secret weapon that will allow us to have a better chance at success."

"We do?"

"Indeed, we do. Nora. Your cousin knows every square inch of the Dietrich mansion and the Langsford Manor next door. She informed me they even have a connecting tunnel which allows easy passage from one estate to the other without having to go out in the elements...handy in the hot, humid summer, I guess."

I'd put on one of the badass outfits my mother had commissioned for us...sort of Lara Croft meets Katniss meets one of the female Avengers. I felt like a rock star whenever I donned one and today was no exception. All blacks and browns and muted purple, with mesh and bits of unknown fabrics that allowed me to move freely, keep me warm—or cool, and had plenty of hiding spots for knives and darts and a few other nifty items.

"Whoa, kiddo. Your eyes have gone black again. It suits you, you know. But you may want to put on your sunglasses so you don't draw attention to yourself."

"I'm tingling, Dorie. I feel different. Alive. Powerful. Like I have a purpose and a right to be here doing whatever I'm meant to do."

"Yep. You definitely are back. You need that ring to remain on you at all times. Here... give me your hand."

Not even questioning what Pandora had planned for me, I held my right hand out toward her. Dorie certainly had me captivated by the magic she began pulsing into my body. I didn't flinch, try to pull away, or question her. I certainly had come a long way in a short matter of minutes.

When Dorie had completed her task, I knew without a doubt that the aquamarine ring would never come off my hand—not without a heap of magic. It gave me comfort and a new sense of confidence on top of the one growing in me already. I shared a brief smile with Pandora, and we hit the road.

"How come I have a feeling we're about to stop back at the diner and pick up a crotchety old witch and my ice queen of a cousin?"

"Because you are an astute witch that knows there is strength in numbers. That, and Adriana will tan our hide if we leave her out of all the fun."

Indeed.

We came to a screeching halt in front of the diner just as Nora and Adriana came out and spied us. Adriana wasted no time in climbing up into the back seat behind Dorie, but Nora hesitated.

"Listen, Lily. I have the map drawn out for both estates and would feel better if I remain out of this part of Dorie's plans. I'm sure she's caught you up on what those are? If I'm to remain undercover and stay in the good graces of both the Dietrich and Langsford clans, it needs to appear that nothing has changed between us," she said diplomatically.

That was fine by me, because until Nora proved her worth and things worked in our favor, nothing *had* changed between us! I'd not trust her so easily just because of a few attempts at reconciliation, not after dealing with the year I've had and the crazy witches running amok with abandon through it.

She must have seen the judgment in my eyes, for she smiled slightly, handed a parcel to Dorie which had the hand-drawn blueprints of the Dietrich and Langsford estate, and turned to leave.

"Thank you for this, Nora. I appreciate it."

What? I too, could be gracious.

After Nora's departure, we continued on our way, but before I could make the turn that would lead us out of the square and in the direction of our enemy's estate, I had to quickly pull over and park. Before either of my companions could protest my sudden inaction, I pointed across the street to what had caught my attention.

Standing in front of the alley between my art warehouse and the mechanic shop was Lorcan and Tiffany. And they were holding hands. I couldn't tell from my position what their conversation might be about, but she was smiling up at him and his body language had me believing he was relaxed and amiable to her company.

"Lily, you're growling. It's going to give you frown lines," Pandora warned.

"I can zap them both from here; just open your back window. I don't know how," said Adriana darkly.

"No. I don't have time for that right now. But I can take care of Tiffany Clarkson by myself."

"Don't be silly. I know you can take care of Tiffany, but we're not about to let you have all the fun!" Adriana cackled then growled herself when Lorcan leaned forward and kissed that wonton hussy on the cheek before wandering back into his shop. It deepened when Tiffany lifted her eyes in our direction and gave us an evil smirk before sauntering over to her chic little Porsche roadster.

How the heck does an officer afford...oh. Wait. Clarkson... of the Sweet Briar Clarksons, who were loaded. Enough said.

I didn't hang around to wait on Tiffany to pass us and leave a trail of fumes in her wake, so I pulled my Jeep back into traffic and made my way around the square heading west. I guess Deputy Clarkson has the day off, otherwise she'd have been in uniform and in her patrol SUV. I felt my jaw tighten and took in a calming breath, letting it out slowly.

"That girl is up to no good, and I have a feeling there is more to it than just getting Lorcan away from you and into her clutches," Adriana surmised. "I'm going to have Susanne look into a few things for me."

"Susanne? Susanne Washington?" I asked.

"Yes. Or Keisha. One of Susanne's nieces works as a maid for the Clarksons. I think it's time we have a little birdie on the inside in that household. They've become far too vocal against our family as of late, and I wonder how close Maybelle is to Stella Langsford Plank. We need Spooky to help us. Where is that ghost anyway?" grumbled Adriana.

"Edith was here the day that crazy homeless man came into my yard, but she was hovering and being distracting, and I may have upset her when I showed my displeasure. She hasn't been around since," I explained. "I feel bad because I didn't mean to scold her...I was just distracted by the weird man and Dorie hanging on to him. The last thing I needed was Edith flying around trying to smack him on the head."

"I hope you didn't hurt her feelings so badly she left for good!" exclaimed Adriana.

"Oh, gosh! I hope not. I didn't mean anything by it."

"Well, I certainly hope she hasn't left either. We need her on the inside giving us aid. Her family compound is massive as are both homes. Try calling her to us, will you?"

I did just that for the better part of the next ten minutes to no avail. No Edith. And no hint she'd heard me. I'd have to worry about her hurt feelings later, however, as we'd just arrived at the back entrance—the service entrance—to the Dietrich and Langsford estates. Although it should really be Dietrich and Plank estates, but poor Arthur Plank was overshadowed by his wife and her family, just as Boris Langsford deferred to his wife, Wilhelmina, and her Dietrich clan. So, the compound was known locally as the Dietrich and Langsford estates.

"Granny, do you think there is a tie between Stella and... Maybelle, did you say? Is that Tiffany's mother?" I asked.

"Yes. Maybelle and Stella went to school together but were never friendly. As a matter of fact, if I am remembering correctly, they were rivals. I would think they'd be cordial but aloof toward each other. You never know, however, because they have a similar goal—knocking us off our pedestal and taking our place."

Ah, the enemy of my enemy and all that.

"The thing is, who would wind up at the top of the heap? I can't see either family conceding to the other." Adriana frowned then pointed to a figure running across the lawn in the distance. "Isn't that the homeless man?"

"Where? Oh! It certainly looks like him but...oh no! Look!"

Much to my horror and dismay, I watched as a stream of greenish magic came out of the woods to our right and flew into the receding figure of the man. He couldn't outrun the magic fast enough, and we watched as he was lifted high into the air then slammed down to the ground. Hard.

He didn't move again after that.

❦ 12 ❧

Unfortunately for Heathcliff Fitzwillow, none of us could get involved other than to call the police station anonymously. And much to my surprise, it was done from a burner phone Pandora had. Like seriously? A crossroads demon had a burner. What was she... a criminal? Forget I asked that.

We had our hands full driving off into the woods on a cut-through that delivery people used, which joined several estates in the area, when we discovered what had attacked Heathcliff. Demons! Demons were in the woods...or that was the consensus from Pandora. Adriana shouted when she saw the forms flying toward the woods and instructed me to follow along that back road, making sure we kept them in our sights but to get far enough away from the estate, considering it would be swarming with police shortly.

"Demons? I don't understand why demons would be wandering around the Dietrich property and why they'd attack Heathcliff. Then again, why would Heathcliff even be out here unless Wilhelmina hired him," I wondered. And seriously...what homeless guy is named Heathcliff? I thought this to myself, belatedly. I mean, his name sounded like a character out of a fantasy novel.

"Do you remember what Nora said? About feeling evil and seeing things out there? Well, those dark forms running around the woods are memory demons. They attack and silently mess up your memories, destroy your convictions...horrible little beasts, even if they are kin in a way to me," stated Dorie.

Memory demons?

"What I find disturbing is they are usually peaceful. Mischief is their game...not attacking humans. But I just witnessed them use magic on that Heathcliff dude. I grabbed my bow earlier to come out here and have a little fun with them and get you some practice in combat. But now? Now we need to hunt them down and take one in for questioning. Adriana, I think you might need to remain here in the Jeep because the woods can be tricky terrain, and you aren't dressed for fighting. I don't want you to get hurt."

We both heard a deep throaty laugh coming from the back seat that sounded like a stone mausoleum being opened, and Adriana leaned forward between the bucket seats. "You are a funny one, aren't you? Watch and learn kids."

With that, the woman I had known for a short time who I understood was a powerful witch, but had suspected her days of glory were over, showed us why she was so feared in these parts by so many people.

Climbing down slowly and carefully from the back seat, Adriana took a few unsteady steps away from the Jeep, then turned to us with a wicked gleam in her eyes. It was chilly but not overly so, probably in the high 50s, so I was not overly concerned when she began to remove her cloak. However, what was under her cloak had me gobsmacked.

Adriana had on an outfit similar to mine but in the darkest blood red, almost black in some areas. She had open-finger leather gloves that looked like second skin and had not one, not two, but three long thin wands attached across her front. There was a nasty, long dagger attached to her side and one barely noticeable tucked in her combat boots.

The combat boots didn't surprise me—she always walked around town in those to give her some height and make her look badass.

Well, she certainly looked the part now.

She was about to open her mouth and blow us a loud raspberry, when a dark form came flying out of the woods behind her and pounced. A demon! I shouted out a warning, but it died on my lips when Adriana, not even turning around to acknowledge the flying creature hurling its way toward her at top speed, reached up and snatched it out of the air. The now-shrieking being tried to escape but to no avail...Adriana flicked it to her left then toasted it.

All that was left was a smoldering pile of ash.

"She's never going to let me live this down, suggesting she's too old for this, is she?" said Dorie in resignation.

"You know it," I replied.

"To your left! Three of them!"

We'd been ducking and dodging and fighting demons going on the better part of twenty minutes now with no end in sight. I was concerned Adriana might not be able to keep up but needn't have bothered—the woman was amazing, in her element, and having a blast. Literally.

Adriana employed a mixture of lightning and explosive magic and kept frying the demons, despite our attempts at capturing one to question. None would give us the opportunity, and all were going at this battle like zealots on a mission to convert. In other words, it didn't look like we'd be speaking with one of them anytime soon.

"Watch it, Lily. There are two more in those trees behind you," shouted Dorie.

"There's one coming up...oof! Hey!" I spun and slammed magic into a tiny bugger who froze in place, and I hoped to keep him alive, but he burst into a million pieces and disintegrated into ashy nothingness. "Oops. Ah, well. Onward."

Pandora was amazing herself. Twisting, blasting, and using her magical bow...I wanted to sit back and watch her technique, but knew I'd wind up a small pile of ash myself if the demons had their way with me. I was astounded when the ridiculous outfit Pandora had on slowly transmuted seemingly of its own accord, leaving Dorie in a liquid black material that resembled a second skin. Seriously, it looked like someone spray-painted latex on her naked body, allow her to move in catlike fashion, impeded by nothing—but protected from many of the attempts at harm by the demons. I just couldn't understand where they were all coming from until Adriana shouted something about a doorway.

"A doorway? Like...to another plane?"

"Of course, to another plane, dummy! Do you think these things roam around Georgia all the time?" she snarked. I let it go...she was in a foul mood because one smallish demon managed to bite her ankle before she did away with him. It had to smart.

Suddenly an arrow whizzed past my face, and I barely managed to hold in a scream.

"Sorry! Big guy behind you."

I turned just as a larger-than-what-we'd-been-dealing-with demon came crashing down to land at my feet. This one didn't disintegrate or turn into an ash pile. Instead, he shuddered a little and rolled over, yellow eyes wide with pain and teeth bared in anger. Thankfully, he seemed paralyzed by the arrow sticking out of him. Wicked ran over and began to paw at his wound.

"Gotcha!" cried Dorie. "Stunner!"

I hesitated briefly, intending to call out to Wicked to stay out of the fracas, but she was having so much fun torturing the demons, I didn't have the heart. I mean, how often does a magical cat get to sit on the chest of a diabolical creature and stare into its eyes while batting the arrow poking up out of it? She was in her element as well.

Adriana took off to our left, yelling she'd take care of the doorway and to hang on to the big demon until she returned. I was only slightly worried, but after watching her in action, I realized there was more to that old witch than I surmised. I was proud of her!

I took out four more smallish demons and Dorie handled three, and then everything quieted down. I made a move to follow where my great-grandmother had headed, but she came trudging down the small hill wiping her hands on her hips, a broad smile on her face.

"I haven't had this much fun in fifty years or so! We need to do this more often, ladies!"

"I take it the doorway is closed?" I asked.

"Locked, sealed, and vanished. I can't believe they opened a portal. Really, Pandora, you need to have a word with your boss. We can't have minor demons popping in whenever they want!" scolded Adriana.

"That's just it... they can't. Someone on this side had to have summoned them. And if I had to guess, I'd say Wilhelmina might be behind it!" replied Dorie. "Although is she that crafty? I don't know. Dealing with demons isn't like summoning a pixie or a troll."

"Who else could it be?" argued Adriana.

"Tiffany," I said with so much conviction I surprised even myself. "Think about it. Her, 'the devil is in the details,' comment, and other such references recently. I don't know how to go about proving it, but it has to be Tiffany."

"Or is it due to her close proximity to Lorcan that's clouding your judgment?" asked Adriana, rubbing her chin in thought.

"I might be holding a grudge, and rightfully so, but you heard her taunting me at Joe's Diner. She's got to be behind all this, but why? And what is the end result?" I pondered while wiping what I suspected might be demon goop off my right arm.

"How about we go wash this mess off and take this demon with us for a little chat," suggested Adriana. "He might spill the beans on who summoned them if we use a little creative torture on him."

Pandora used her magic to lift the demon to a standing position and made to tether his claw-like hands behind his back—but he was waiting for just such a move. The second Pandora eased up on the magic to move his wrists, the demon launched at Adriana, who had no choice but to blast him.

With a loud "splat" the terrible creature was no more.

"Oopsie!" cried Adriana.

Well, that was something you don't get over right away. Although I felt alive. More alive than I'd been feeling as of late. So alive I might have pulled into Lorcan's shop and leaned out my Jeep window to give him a resounding kiss on his parted lips, leaving him a tad breathless but smiling before I pulled my Jeep back out and headed toward home.

Take that, Tiffany Clarkson of the Sweet Briar Clarksons!

"Lily, watch where you're going and get that grin off your face. You look mental." Adriana was riding shotgun with Dorie in the back seat polishing her bow, Wicked by her side. "Don't go to your place, bring me home. I want to check on Antonio and need to get out of this outfit."

"Speaking of outfits. I'm assuming Adelaide had one made for you. It looks an awful lot like mine."

"Only I look better in it. Yes. She commissioned one for me as well," Adriana admitted.

"As for you," I addressed Pandora in my rearview mirror. "Nice getup. That's a handy little trick you have up your sleeve—pun intended."

"It *is* handy. It's why I'm never worried about my clothing choice, nor should I be. I like my fashion sense."

So did every male in these parts. Well, more power to Dorie...she certainly could pull off her "look." Heck, if I had her body, I might run around in skimpy clothing or even naked!

Or not.

Instead of turning down Wildflower Lane, I continued along Main Street heading out of town toward my great-grandmother's Victorian mansion. When I pulled into the drive, I noticed both my parents' cars were in the driveway around back, so I knew they were home. Dad bought himself a new Ford truck and Mom chose a tiny brown MG, all checkerboard decked out and pin-striped, that she'd been zipping around town in. It was beyond nice to see them both living their lives again after their ordeal, and even I had to admit them moving in with Adriana and Antonio had been the wise decision.

Adriana and Antonio had taken the former servants' rooms on the main level and turned it into their apartment with everyone sharing the big kitchen and common areas, while Mom and Dad had the rest of the house. I knew Grandpa Antonio was thrilled to have his grandson home once more.

Charlie and Adelaide could keep an eye on the aging Antonio and had the freedom, in this big, old rambling mansion, to begin turning it into the home they would eventually inherit. In their mid-forties...they'd have decades to grow old in this place! It made me wonder if they'd want to have another child or two—incredulous to ponder, but witches were long-lived and, in the past, many didn't marry and start a family until they were well into their fifties.

Which begged the question, did I want siblings after being the only child?

The age difference alone would be astounding and did some weird things to my brain. What if Charlie and Adelaide did want kids? Would I turn into a jealous older sibling? Not me. I'd be thrilled for them.

Right?

"You can take a shower and borrow some of your mother's things since you both share a size," said Adriana. "I will put some coffee on, and you can join us in the den. Pandora, I assume you can do your thing and be cleaned up of demons bits with a new outfit as well?"

Dorie nodded yes and hopped out of my Jeep, followed by Wicked. By the time her feet touched the ground she appeared fresh from the shower with her hair all shiny and a new—and a rather subdued for Dorie outfit on. Jeans and a fuzzy pink sweater.

Neat trick.

Dashing up the expansive staircase, I met my parents on their way down and explained my current state of disarray. Only mildly alarmed—the benefits of having paranormal parents who'd been through their own ordeal—I mentioned Adriana's request that we meet in the den for coffee, and I hoped snacks of some sort. Fighting demons certainly brings on an appetite.

My life was so bizarre!

I quickly showered and slipped on some jeans and an old Aerosmith sweatshirt Adelaide left out for me on the bed, gathered up my soiled outfit, then clamored down the back staircase and into the laundry room where I set my clothing to wash, hoping the demon gunk wouldn't clog my great-grandparents' pipes.

I was about to leave the kitchen and enter the den when my family's voices reached me, and I paused.

"The Council doesn't care one whit about that. Liliana

used magic again, and they want her pulled in for questioning —now," said Adriana.

"But that is ridiculous! Demons were attacking her! What was she supposed to do, let them harm her?" cried Adelaide.

"Addy, I agree, but Gloria Stillwell was emphatic in her argument that Lily be present tomorrow morning at 10 AM sharp for questioning. I tried pulling every string I could— even Owen has his hands tied."

"We will be there. I am not letting my daughter face the Council and the Order of Origin alone," stated my dad, heatedly. His voice quivered with passion, and I could feel his anger from where I hid behind the swinging door that led to the den.

"Well, that's good in a way...it means Cousin Maggie Fortune will be the representative from the Order," said Adelaide with hope in her voice. "One more on our side."

"Unfortunately, no. Gloria informed me it would be Delvin Fitzwick coming over from Scotland to question Liliana. He is Maggie's superior, and while she has been called in to be here as backup, she isn't in charge. Nor are any of us allowed to contact her before the meeting."

What's with all the Fitz-named people as of late? And Maggie here? I knew I latched onto the mundane to keep things light since my alarm bells were ringing—especially since I knew I was in some deep doo-doo in reality. My distracted thoughts cleared upon Adriana's next words on the matter.

"Delvin is good at what he does—maybe too good. If he feels Liliana is a threat, he will move to nullify her powers despite what that book said. We need to convince him to consider the tome's passage. But will he? Will any of the Elders?"

"So what? Did he just drop everything, hop on a plane, and is even now heading to Georgia?" cried Adelaide.

"No. He was already in New York on business. So, he's flying down tonight and will be waiting on Lily at the Council chamber tomorrow." Adriana sounded weary, and this had me concerned. Not for her health—she proved she was stout with those fighting maneuvers earlier. No, it was for my future I worried. My freedom and ability to perform magic. Things were starting to look bleak. "Maggie, however, had to drop everything and head here...she was supposedly on her way to New Orleans."

"Is Ellie with her, do you know?" I asked, heading in from the den.

"That is a definite no. Before they cut our contact to your cousin, she mentioned something about keeping Ellie and Pandora as far away from each other as possible to limit any damage that may occur." Adriana gave Dorie a wry look—Dorie simpered a little and shrugged as if to say, "What can I do?"

"And we still have no proof it was Tiffany or one of Edith's kin. Has anyone discovered where Edith has run off to? Did you try calling out to her?" asked Dorie, trying to deflect the attention from her recent shenanigans with Ellie.

"I've been trying. Edith isn't responding. I'm not sure I should impel her to appear before me. Edith can be a tad touchy when it comes to summoning, but if it means aiding Liliana, I will," Adriana declared.

"Whatever happened with Tiffany Clarkson and the video footage you captured, Pandora? Did you show it to Sheriff Buford? What did Glen say?" asked Adelaide.

"The good sheriff said Tiffany explained it away by saying she was only confronting the man for being homeless and wandering the streets of Sweet Briar. She didn't know him or hire him—and it must have been convincing because Glen believed her. I mean, what else could he do? She is a Clarkson...they play by different rules around here."

"Are they really that powerful?" I asked.

"Money talks, Squirt. And the Clarksons have it in buckets. Rumor has it they could give the Queen of England a loan," Adriana replied.

I felt something soft on my ankles and looked down to find Wicked weaving in and out, and that's when I noticed another set of feet standing close to mine...or should I say smoky knees. Looking up, I found the ghost of Edith Plank watching me with a solemn face.

"Edith!" I whispered. "Where have you been?"

Holding her fingers to her lips, Edith motioned for me to follow her away from the swinging door—and the possibility of being overheard—and over to the back entrance.

"Lily. You need to get out of here. I just came from my family estate. What a mess! That Heathcliff Fitzwillow dude? He's a goner. My grandmother is insisting you did away with him to keep him from speaking out and proving she had nothing to do with hiring him. I'm starting to think the police believe her—that Tiffany Clarkson sure seemed to believe her."

"That's because Tiffany is behind all of this, Edith. I just need proof. And how can anyone believe I had anything to do with Heathcliff's death!? He was killed by demons!"

"Because Tiffany suggested it was you who summoned them!" Edith responded in a hushed voice.

The nerve of that hussy!

Even more proof in favor of my estimation that she was the guilty party in all of this!

But how do I prove it to everyone else? Especially the Witch Council and the representative from the Order of Origin? I needed to get word to Maggie so I could discover what was being said about me...but with our lines of communication blocked, I didn't have many options.

Unless...

"Edith, I may need you to run interference for me. Are you up for it?"

"You know I am, Lily."

Was Tiffany working alone? Was this yet another way for her to put a wedge between Lorcan and me then swoop in and... what? Steal him away if I languished in the Witch Prison? Did she have enough talent to be the one who'd muddled my thoughts? And once I reasoned that out...had she put some kind of charm on Lorcan? Is that why he seemed enchanted by that vixen? The more I pondered it all, the more something began to tickle my memory, and I knew I had to act quickly.

I needed to give my fiancé the benefit of the doubt—trust had to be the foundation of our relationship and future—but I also knew I should speak with him. I also needed fodder to prove my theory, and I didn't know what I should do next. Or did I?

"Edith...can you get to Pandora without anyone else seeing you?"

"How can I do that? The minute I try to sneak in there, Adriana will see me."

I'm on it.

I jumped at least ten feet when Wicked's voice tickled my senses and entered my thoughts. Before I could react, my cat slinked across the kitchen and slipped into the den. I knew within minutes Dorie would be by my side, so I slipped outside quietly, heading over to my Jeep to wait, Edith on my heels.

I'd have to assess how I felt about the novel turn of events with Wicked when the current mess was over. Right now, I could barely process her voice entering my thoughts while dealing with everything else.

"Can I help you, Lily? I can be your lookout or whatever you might need."

"Of course, Edith, but more than that, I need to get word to Cousin Maggie. I know she will be able to see and hear you —Ellie and all that. Can you find out where she is and what the dirt is on me? What are the grievances? I am sure there is a vast list of transgressions, and I need to be able to debate and fight with knowledge and not get blindsided with anything. With you and Dorie...and Wicked, of course, we will get to the bottom of this and save the day. Or my bacon anyway!"

It felt good to have my friends with me, fighting for me. And I had to pause when reflecting on my team. Edith and Pandora. Two unlikely companions who I now considered my besties. Who would have thought it would turn out this way?

Once Dorie materialized with Wicked in her wake, I explained to my team just what needed to be done to capture our culprit.

"But first, I need to stop by Lorcan's shop again."

❧ 14 ❧

If my family wondered where Pandora and I had gotten to, they didn't come running to find out. Perhaps Adriana, suspecting I had something up my sleeve as well, kept everyone out of my way and crossed her fingers, hoping for the best. It certainly was a vote of confidence that everyone didn't show up en masse to put out my fires, and I appreciated it.

Of course, at this point, they may have just washed their hands of me and hoped I'd come out fine in the end...but I doubt it. If there is one thing positive I can say about my Dolce and Croy clan, it's that they stick together. I mean...look at Cousin Nora making a complete attitude adjustment. Who would have thought that could happen?

I drove as fast as I dared, hoping no police would see my Jeep and decide I needed to be held until my appearance at the Council tomorrow, but I managed to get us to the relative safety of Lorcan's shop without hindrance.

Edith departed as soon as we were on our way, and I hoped she discovered Maggie's whereabouts—and my cousin was willing to share information that would aid me. I don't know Maggie all that well, even though we had met a few times now, and I didn't know if going against the Order would be something she'd be down with.

"Dorie, do me a favor and follow my lead. Don't warn Lorcan about anything or try to explain. He is either going to pick up my signals, or he really is under Tiffany's spell."

"I don't understand though, Lily. What exactly are you hoping to accomplish?" asked Dorie.

"A little Pandora-style mischief. You know, shake things up a little," I stated with a smug little smirk.

Pandora grinned and winked at me, and I pulled into an empty stall. We hopped out and sauntered over to the counter where Lorcan was sitting, feet propped up on his desk, on the phone with an apparent customer. Wicked remained in my Jeep, stretched out on the dashboard, watching our every move. Lorcan smiled at me quizzically and nodded at Pandora who glared at him. He arched an eyebrow in my direction, but I just smiled blandly.

"OK, Dan, I understand. These things happen. I'll be here when you decide to do the work."

Lorcan hung up and made to stand, but I stopped him by holding up my hand, palm facing outward.

"Sounds like you lost another customer. Perhaps you should run over and tell Tiffany while she's showering. I mean, how else could she possibly know your business is in a slump? Or perhaps you wait until you're in that afterglow of pillow talk for all I know."

"Lily...what the heck? How could you think that of me?" Lorcan slowly slid back down onto his chair and frowned.

"Oh, look. Now the great empath is all hurt. I've also been informed you wouldn't last long being married to such an evil witch. When it came down to it, letting the town of Sweet Briar—heck, the world even—suffer under my malevolence would drain you to the point you have to choose to walk away or do away with me. For the good of all."

"Lily, I don't know who or what happened to…"

"Furthermore, I have been summoned to appear at the Witch Council tomorrow morning. I would prefer you remain as far away from the circus as possible. I'm no longer holding you to our banns. We are through, Lorcan. Over. Finished. You are free. What I need now is a multiple-trick pony…and they don't exist. Don't try to call me—I won't pick up. Don't try to make any further contact…not with me."

I finished my statement with a long penetrating stare to an open-mouthed Lorcan, then spun on my heels and returned to my Jeep. Climbing inside, I barely waited for Dorie to follow and tore out of the shop like a madwoman. Lorcan would either get the assignment or fail miserably…I could only hope for the best.

"I assume you suspect Tiffany has that shop bugged in some way?" asked Dorie.

"That has to be how she keeps finding out about stuff. And it would be easy for her to accomplish. Right now, she is probably doing a happy victory dance. I can't wait to rain on her parade. And she must be listening in on Lorcan's phone calls…I hope he doesn't try calling me."

"But how?"

"That's the million-dollar question, Dorie."

"He's going to show up tomorrow. You know that, right?" stated Dorie.

"I know. I just hope he's on his toes because we have no idea what is about to go down, and I need a miracle. Hopefully, it will come riding in on a multi-trick pony."

My phone dinged, and I glanced down to find a text from Nora. *Tiffany has been assigned to guard the Witch Council chamber room tonight. She is there now with two of her underlings. Not sure what this means but thought you should know her whereabouts.*

I tapped my fingers on my steering wheel and briefly considered heading to the Council to confront Tiffany. But to what end? That choice would be folly. I needed to figure out more about what being a Sweet Briar Witch really meant.

I didn't know what to do next and considered heading home to brainstorm with Dorie, when I received an unexpected phone call from Doreen and Donald Murphy. My, but I'm popular.

"Lily. Oh, good! We caught you. Donald and I are at a loss on what to do about a little situation and hoped you could help us before we are forced to call the sheriff. Please, Lily. Head on over here if you can."

I loved Doreen and Donald, but I was kind of in a time crunch here and didn't know if I could drop everything to help with whatever issue they had.

"I might not be the right person to call, Doreen. I'm not sure if you've heard, but the Witch Council has me in their crosshairs. And..."

"No. Lily, please. It has something to do with the man that died. We don't want to discuss this on the phone. Just get here quick," said Doreen, then she disconnected the call.

"How do you like that? Doreen wants me to go to their motel and it has something to do with the homeless man. Why would Doreen and Donald know anything about him?" I asked.

"I guess we will find out soon enough," replied Dorie.

Pandora had been working on some notes she'd scribbled down, trying to piece everything we knew together to try and make some sense out of it all and tie events. Nothing seemed to make sense and time was ticking.

"You know, the only thing that keeps jumping at me is Tiffany. I know we want her for this, and that's what I'm working on, but she passed Sheriff Glen's scrutiny when she claimed she'd only confronted the homeless Heathcliff and told him to move along out of town. Now, we blamed Wilhelmina Dietrich originally due to the long history of discord between your family and hers. But what if it is Tiffany Clarkson? How do we prove she is behind this? She is a witch...but does she have enough power to summon demons? And why? Why have them attack Heathcliff Fitzwillow in the first place? What was he doing on Dietrich property? Why was he in town? Who is the mystery woman that hired him to confront and antagonize you? And why?"

Pandora wasn't asking me per se, she was working things out, adding notes, and connecting dots, leaving me to ponder things on my own. But she had brought up some stellar arguments. What did tie all these things together? And more importantly, who had it in for me to this degree that caused the unexpected facing of the music of my purported actions and a possible vote tomorrow morning at the Witch Council?

And who the heck was Heathcliff Fitzwillow anyway? Where did he come from? And that name! It should come up in the search engines being so unique, yet after a cursory glance yesterday, I found nothing. Not one speck or hint of anything. He was an enigma!

I made a U-turn and drove as quickly as I dared to the Murphy's motel on the outskirts of town, pulling into the paved parking lot that led to each individual room. I didn't have to search for my friends; they were standing outside of Room 20 looking perplexed.

Hopping out of my Jeep, with Wicked on my heels, I ambled around the front and over to my dear friends who looked relived when they saw me pulling in.

"Hey, guys. What's up?"

"Oh, Lily! Thank goodness you're here. It's this Fitzwillow business. We aren't quite sure what to do now that he's been murdered," cried Doreen.

Donald shook his head, pulling in his bottom lip, his face a picture of concern.

"Bad business that. And now we are stuck in the middle of it all."

I was beyond confused. "I don't understand. Why does it concern either one of you? He was a homeless man passing through town. And while I am upset and find it deplorable someone targeted him causing his death, it has nothing to do with you."

"Oh, but it does! Why would you say he was homeless? That nice man was here on business—or so he said. Something about some classified work he couldn't speak of, but he needed a place to stay on the down-low for a few days. Now, we find he's been murdered, and he's left his belongings here in this room. Only, we're afraid to call the sheriff—what if he arrests us for concealing evidence?" asked Donald.

"Concealing evidence? Hang on a minute...he was here on business? Heathcliff Fitzwillow? But...but he was a homeless man wandering around town! I found him in my yard peering in my windows!"

"Homeless? Oh no. Not Heathcliff. He said he was just in from his head office here on a business matter that needed to be kept under the strictness confidence. We assured him we wouldn't tell a soul he was staying here. His references checked out, after all. Did we do something wrong?" cried Doreen.

"Sheriff Buford is going to come down hard on us, I just know it. What if he was a criminal...or worse? This isn't good," lamented Donald.

"Is this the room here?" asked Dorie. "Can we go in and have a look around?"

"That's why I called you, Lily. I figured...well, with the amount of trouble you are in, dear, we figured what's one more mark on your record?" Doreen looked at me apologetically.

I couldn't blame the Murphys for their reasoning. I mean, I am the town menace, after all.

"Let's head in, shall we?" I said as a response, curious as to what we'd find in Heathcliff's room.

I slipped on a pair of gloves—don't ask me why I carry them around in my vehicle ready for action—so as not to leave fingerprints, and I suggested Dorie do the same. She just created hers out of thin air.

Entering Room 20, the first thing to hit me was how neat and tidy it was. The bed had obviously been slept in but was made. Clothes were folded on one chair. His suitcase and what I assumed was a spare jacket was neatly tucked into the closet. In the bathroom, the man's toiletries were lined up and looked new, as if he'd bought them for travel and not grabbed used items from home. Wicked padded over to the wastebasket in the corner of the room and sniffed around, but it was empty.

The one surprising find was the man's wallet inside a briefcase, and what I found there left me in stunned realization that not all was as it seemed.

"Heathcliff Fitzwillow is—was—I mean, not what he seemed! He was..."

"...An agent in the Order of Origin," finished Edith, who'd materialized.

"Who is he, dear?" asked Doreen. Neither she nor Donald were aware of Edith's appearance.

"An agent of the Order of Origin. Holy cow...this just went from bad to worse."

"And how," said Dorie.

"But what does that mean, Lily? What does that have to do with...oh." Realization dawned with Donald a split second before it caught up with Doreen.

"Yeah. The man sent to obviously spy on me winds up dead after I confront him, and he just happens to be with the Order? I'm in deep trouble. Like...massively deep trouble here," I said glumly.

"There's more I have to tell you, Lily. But right now, you need to get out of here and back to the library. Like now. Before the sheriff finds you," urged Edith.

I didn't question Edith in front of Doreen and Donald, who I'd assured were not in any kind of danger with the authorities. I suggested they call the sheriff and explain about Heathcliff and that I couldn't stick around to help because of my current status.

The three of us rushed back to my Jeep and pulled out into traffic, heading back to Sweet Briar.

"Why the library?" I asked Edith. "What did you find out?"

"Well, I spoke with Maggie, and she said the Council is freaked out with this Sweet Briar Witch issue regarding you and that Tarni Vanderzee. There is a surprise visitor who accompanied Delvin Fitzwick, but Maggie isn't sure who she is. With ties to you, Maggie isn't allowed much say in the goings-on, and she is livid. Like, whoa, I'd heard redheads have legendary tempers, but Maggie's is off the chart. Oh, and she has words for you, Pandora. Ellie is not with her, and it has something to do with keeping the two of you apart, "for your own good and the safety of all." I'm sure you know what that's about."

Pandora rolled her lips to keep from laughing, all the while giving me an innocent look when I glared at her.

"But what did you find out?" I asked again, trying to steer the conversation back to where I needed it to be.

"Maggie stated there was a hint about the Sweet Briar Witch that could only be spoken if one properly asked the Black Grimoire a very specific question. Before it was on the radar that you might be this entity, Maggie was in on the developments surrounding this case, and knows what to ask!"

Well, that was good, I guess. Now we could go to the library and what? Fight my Fairy Godfather, Jerry and not gain entry probably.

"Off to the library it is!" I cried, hoping for the best.

"This is going to be hopeless," I said, realizing belatedly I had to give a blood tribute to that damned door. "Look at it, leering at me all smug."

"You have to cut yourself, Lily. We need to get in," chided Dorie sympathetically.

"But I don't want to! I hate this."

Get over it! You're a dark witch, a siren, a vampire, and a demon, not to mention whatever else you have running through your veins! Use your vampire teeth and scrape your hand—you won't feel a thing! Sheesh!

I jumped twenty feet then looked down at Wicked who blinked lazily up at me. Her eyes were gleaming behind that calm demeanor, and I knew she had entered my thoughts. And *sheesh?* Really?

"Dorie, if I use my vampire abilities, my fangs," I whispered tentatively, "will it hurt? Do you know if I'd feel it?"

"Well, duh! I should have thought of that! Of course, you won't feel it. Vampires open their wrists and such to feed younglings all the time. Go for it."

I walked over to the demon door who I was certain

expected more whining from me, but I really wanted those days of kvetching and complaining to be behind me. If I planned on taking on the Witch Council, the Order of Origin, and Tiffany Clarkson, I needed a backbone to beat all backbones.

Holding open my palm, I watched in abject satisfaction as the look of shock overcame the demon when I channeled my inner vampire and my fangs descended. Running a fang across my palm did indeed draw blood, and I barely noticed a slight sting. I slowly raised my eyes, playfully, filled with a sudden rush of witchy satisfaction and impish mischief and instead of offering it to him, I dipped my free finger into the pool of blood and tapped the demon on the nose. The door popped open.

"Excellent," I chuckled, and sashayed into the library beyond. My mirth was cut short when the trio of library assistants looked up in shock and dismay, then surrounded me before I could proceed further.

Filbert and his two female consorts stopped me cold and began protesting in earnest.

"Oh no you don't, Lily Sweet. You are not to take one step further."

"Leave. You must go, now!"

"You are still a persona non grata! Leave!" shouted Filbert.

"Stop showing off with your Latin utterings, Filbert, and get out of my way. I need to talk to that book again."

"No! I won't allow it. Mister Jerry isn't here, and I am in charge. You shall not pass!"

"Who are you, Gandalf? I most certainly shall pass. This is a matter of utmost importance."

Filbert wasn't impressed and snapped his fingers at his minions. The two female whatever the heck these are, flew across the room and launched themselves at me. With no time to spare to this insanity, I quickly called up my magic and... nothing. Pandora, sensing my ire, flicked her hand in the trio's direction and froze them in place.

Quickly swallowing my spark of magic, I took a steadying breath and thanked Dorie—who probably saved my hide, considering any magic would have the Council descending with gusto to arrest me.

We quickly maneuvered through the desks to get to the doorway where Jerry had earlier retrieved the book, and entered the next room. That was a miscalculation of epic proportion when we found ourselves overrun by pixies.

"Gah! Dorie! Quick...freeze them or evaporate them. Do something because...ow! They bite!"

"I'm trying, but they don't seem to want to listen to me. Chuck is my friend, but this group is a little touchy."

Probably because they are as irritated with Pandora as Maggie. Just what did Ellie and Pandora get up to a few weeks ago? I didn't have time for that, almost letting loose my magic, despite the repercussions, when like a flash of lightning, Wicked came to the rescue. Snarling and spitting, my fearless feline became a whirling dervish, tearing across the room and leaving a cowering and fearful pack of petrified pixies in her wake.

One by one, the pixies shrunk to the tiny Tinkerbell formations and hid behind a pile of books. With Wicked on guard, tail swishing and whiskers twitching, I managed to reach the shelf with the Black Grimoire and pulled it down and over to a table to examine. It didn't seem to be awake as it had been previously, and I wasn't sure what to do next.

"Any ideas, ladies?" I asked.

"Try calling to it or speaking. Maybe if you directly address it, something will happen," suggested Dorie.

"I think you need to tell it you need help, Lily. That is what Maggie suggested. And another thing. I have been hanging around my family estate. I'm not sure my family is involved in any of this other than waiting and hoping you'll be voted out of the Council permanently and casting their vote in favor of nullifying your magic. Other than that? The talk around the compound has been one of intrigue. My grandmother doesn't understand what is causing your magic to go haywire, and she is amazed you aren't the powerhouse they feared you would be. Does that sound like someone who has been behind all of this? I think not," said Edith with a frown. "In any case, I think you need to just call out to the book and see what happens."

I hesitantly placed my hands on the cover of the old book and sighed. Then I squared my shoulders and with authority and commanded the book to heed my call. "I need your aid. I have something to ask of you," I stated with as much bravado as I could muster. Surprisingly, the book stirred at my words and began to quiver.

Removing my hands quickly, I nevertheless remained close to the tome and awaited its response.

"Lily Sweet, back for more? I thought I told you all before."

"Hey! Stop rhyming, that was my gig," cried Dorie.

Chuckling in a deep voice that sounded like an old crow on its last legs, the book opened and began to let its pages slowly turn while it continued its query.

"What is it you want of me this time, Lily Sweet?"

"I have a very specific question I need to ask you, if I may."

Edith whispered the question in my ear, and I drew back, giving her a quizzical look, but she only nodded, prodding me to ask the tome.

"Book, is the secret about the Sweet Briar Witch the fact that anyone with dark witch and two other Breed lineage has the ability and power to become one?"

"Why indeed, that is true. Sweet Briar Witches used to be

common in antediluvian times, but then pure-blooded Breed became jealous, banning interbreeding, which caused a shortage of Sweet Briar witchfolk...and the lore became lost and altered over time."

Edith whispered another question into my ear then backed away slightly.

"Book, do I create magic by using the blossoms of the rose bushes that bear the same name? And the rose hips?"

"That is the greatest secret of all, Lily Sweet. Only a Sweet Briar Witch can create powerful magic by using the shrub...but an even greater secret—the most powerful magic comes from the thorns. Use that and you control the most formidable of the arcane arts."

"Flurb Fweet! Deez gurp! Deez!" One of the wee pixies began to chatter at us, causing Pandora's face to blanch.

"What do you mean, Flora? Who was here?"

"Deez! Hood, ah hoodie. Flurb!"

"Describe her."

The little pixie Dorie addressed as Flora rolled her eyes and stamped her foot. Then she pointed and me and continued her wee tirade.

"Zeebot! Zeep, zeep. Neeve ang deez. GURP!"

The book began to rumble and quiver with every tiny utterance, and Pandora looked concerned, then angry, before thanking the pixie and turning to me with cold, blank eyes.

"Tiffany was down here looking up potions in the Fuchsia Grimoire."

"And...?"

"Lily. The Fuchsia Grimoire is a vile book."

"Seriously? I would think this one here, no disrespect, Book, would be the foul one. But fuchsia? It sounds more like something Jerry would use for decorating or some such."

The Black Grimoire snorted with glee.

"No, Lily. Out of all the books in this particular Forbidden Library, the Fuchsia Grimoire is by far the worst."

Well, OK. But it didn't help me if Pandora would only speak in headlines and not give me the nitty-gritty. I felt like I spent most of my time trying to prompt everyone to continue the story, and I was running out of precious time.

"And? Dorie...you have to give me more here! I need to know what Tiffany was looking for."

"But that's just it. We can't ask the Fuchsia Grimoire like we can the Black. The Fuchsia Grimoire demands an in-between, someone who acts as a conduit of sorts in which messages are relayed. It's a blood tribute."

"So, what does that mean? Did Tiffany sacrifice someone to the book?" I asked in frustration.

"More like, someone here's duties also entail being that conduit, and if I'm not mistaken, I know who that might be," smiled Dorie evilly.

❀

"No! I will not, and you can't make me," cried Filbert in alarm.

"Oh, but we can," I insisted, tired of this pompous little twit. Filbert had wasted another precious thirty minutes protesting and posturing until I'd finally had enough and reached out to throttle him. But that's when one of the female assistants ran over and beseeched me to reconsider.

"I will show you the book. Please don't hurt Filbert. I failed miserably and let that witch in here. Filbert is covering for me because...um...we are friends," she ended lamely.

"You're sweet on each other!" cried Dorie. "And here old Filbert is trying to pretend he's a by-the-book, upstanding employee, but he is obviously covering for your massive mistake, uh...what is your name anyway?"

"Clarice."

"Well, Clarice, I assume what you did was a bad thing. Otherwise, you wouldn't be so wrung out about it, am I right?" Dorie smelled something fishy and went on the attack. Filbert, literally went on the attack, and began bouncing around doing some kind of boxing moves, thrusting, and jabbing and looking the fool. Did he think Pandora would begin a fighting match with him? Or run from his power display of sheer idiocy?

He kept making little "Hmpf" and "Huh," sounds as he bobbed and weaved, and it didn't surprise me one bit when Dorie landed a left hook that sent the little guy hurtling through space until he landed in a heap across the room. She never even looked at Filbert, keeping her eyes locked on Clarice.

Filbert moaned, but wisely remained on the ground and away from Pandora.

Clarice shrieked and covered her mouth, and the other female assistant fainted. Lovely. Now we'd be accused of library assistant abuse. I still had no idea what these slight beings were, nor did I really care, if you got right down to it.

"Listen Clarice, I need to know what Deputy Clarkson was looking up. Did she inform you to keep your mouth shut about her being here?"

The little woman nodded in the affirmative and began to sob loudly.

"Stop that, Clarice. I need you to trust that I am trying to do good for this town, and Deputy Clarkson might have something horrible up her sleeve." But why? I had no idea. Unless it was a way to take me out of competition, I had no idea why this fixation on me.

"I will tell you, but you have to promise not to get Filbert in trouble. Don't let him take the fall for me."

"That's not up to us, Clarice. Pandora and I won't say

anything to anyone—least of all Jerry—if you'd just hurry up and tell me what Tiffany did down here."

Clarice didn't look convinced at my words, but what choice did she have, really? Approaching me and skirting around the looming form of Dorie—now who's posturing? — Pandora grinned menacingly but didn't hinder the slight woman from coming to stand in front of me.

"I have to place my hands on your temples, and you will see and hear all."

"Don't you dare try anything funny, toots, or I will turn your boyfriend into a pile of ash," warned Dorie. Clarice gulped and nodded her understanding then reached out and gently placed her fingertips on either side of my face.

Instantly, I could see the Fuchsia Grimoire lying open on a table before me as my hands—no, Tiffany's hands—furiously turned the pages until she reached the passage she was hunting for. And I groaned in dismay when I read it.

"Holy cow, Dorie. She looked up how to make a mass poison that will wipe out at least fifty people instantly the minute they breathe it in. Any remaining people will get a weaker hit as the magic gas dissipates quickly, but even they will have permanent nerve damage and lesser magical ability. Permanently!"

"Did she just look it up for kicks, or is she planning something?" Dorie wondered aloud.

Edith was wringing her hands, then flew over to me to get my attention. "Lily! You don't think Tiffany is planning an attack on the Witch Council tomorrow do you?"

"But why? To what end?" I wondered.

We all remained deeply lost in our thoughts while horrible visions danced in our heads. What could Tiffany's plans be? Why would she purposely attack the Council? Unless...

"Tiffany is going to taunt me or do something to provoke me into action, hoping I will release my wonky magic and have it be a distraction so she can release this horrible poison. She's going to make it look like I did this. Oh my gosh, Dorie. She is going to kill an entire roomful of people and pin it on me!"

"We are going to stop her before she gets the chance to do anything!" said Dorie.

"How?"

"I don't know, but I need to answer this text."

"From?"

"Your fiancé, I presume. Especially since it says, *This is Lorcan, I'm texting from Stu's phone. We need to talk.*"

It worked. Lorcan understood the assignment, and how!

I opened my mouth to have Pandora expound further, but just then the Fuchsia Grimoire cleared its throat—if they even have throats—and began to speak.

"If I may have a minute of your time, Lily Sweet. I believe we need to get to know one another better."

I'm not sure of much right now, but I do know things are about to get mighty interesting.

❧ 16 ❧

They say you have to let things go sometimes and have faith.

They say to trust in the greater good. That *good will always defeat evil in the end* is the foundation to base one's actions and how to focus one's thoughts.

They say to manifest your reality because what you think will be.

I still don't know who "they" are, but my thoughts were in a mosh pit getting pummeled by manifestations of chaos and doom. I'd already bitten my thumbnail down to nothing and began working on the other. I even yelled at Wicked who'd been weaving in and around my ankles like an ice-skater doing figure eights with the fervor of a Bible-thumper at a biker rally. A clothing-optional biker rally. I assumed Wicked felt my emotions, and it made her reactive.

In other words, I was a train wreck of doubt, so my cat was wacky!

My nerves had a lot to do with the fact that my friends had abandoned me. Edith took off to spy on Tiffany and the two agents she had helping her patrol the Witch Council overnight. Pandora told me to sit tight at home, that she had a ton of things to do before tomorrow, and she'd get back to me when she had it all figured out. I protested loudly, mind you, that I should be in on whatever she'd cooked up, but Dorie insisted it involved magic, and I had to stay far away from anything that smacked of the arcane—despite the very witchy thing I'd done a few minutes ago without anyone but me the wiser. But I digress. I needed my peeps around me and didn't like that I was alone. Even my cousin Andrea had abandoned me. Back at school this week, I felt bereft and lonely, despite my cat trying her best to calm me.

"Speaking of calming, listen you," I addressed my inky black feline, "What's with the ESP, voice in my head, woo-woo stuff, huh?"

Wicked stopped weaving and sat, blinking up at me like she didn't understand a word I was saying to her. I knew better.

"So, can we talk? Is it something that just happens? Or can you turn it on and off at will? What?"

Wicked continued to lazy blink up at me, and I had to retrain myself from strangling her.

"Look, it's just you and me here, all alone. There is no one to witness our conversation. Why don't you just tell me what the deal is?"

"I don't know what you mean. Deal? I was just sorting through my seeds is all," said a voice from my mudroom.

"Jumping Jehoshaphat! Abner! You scared the bejesus out of me! What are you doing here?"

"Weren't you just speaking to me, Lily?" Abner came wandering in from my mudroom, a picture of confusion as he pulled on his bottom lip with one hand and scratched his head with the other.

"No, I wasn't speaking to you! I was...I mean..." Not wanting to admit I was asking my cat questions, fully expecting her to answer me, I decided it would be prudent to change the subject. "Seeds? Isn't it a little early to pull out seeds for a garden? We're in the middle of January," I asked, despite the fact that I'd been busy doing a little pruning not twenty minutes ago. But no one knew this but me. I glanced down at my coffee table and the evidence of my gardening but tried to focus on Abner's words.

"Well, no. Not really. I like to go through last year's seeds and make sure nothing has molded over or gone bad in other ways. Then I like to plot out the garden bed and count the seeds to see how much I can start in the greenhouse by February. Got to get a jump on things down here in the south!"

"I thought you were working on the greenhouse with Lorcan?" I asked.

"Well, yeah. But he's busy tonight."

"I think Pandora is pestering him about now, is that what you mean?"

"No. Pandora might have gone a-lookin' for Lorcan, but he's busy helping that Tiffany Clarkson. She had to hire two agents to help her patrol the Council building...and Lorcan is one of her men."

I guess Abner realized how weird that sounded and how upsetting the news would be to me, because he blushed red and made quick excuses as to why he suddenly needed to rush out of my home and back to his little cabin beyond the shrub hedge.

I was stunned.

Lorcan was working with Tiffany?

Don't believe a word of it. Trust him and trust your friends to help.

"Oh, now you are going to talk?" I glanced down at Wicked, then jumped when another voice entered my space.

"Talk? I haven't said one word. What's wrong with you, Liliana?"

Adriana waltzed into my den like she owned the place and plopped down in one of my club chairs. "What's with you, glum-puss?"

"Seriously? I am about to lose my fiancé, my magic, and my standing in this town, and you are wondering why I am glum?"

"You are not about to lose anything. Not if I have a say in things—which I do."

"Well, you are right about that. I am not going down without a fight. This is baloney and these trumped-up charges have no merit. It seems like The Order of Origin and the Witch Council are shooting blind. They have no idea what a Sweet Briar Witch is, and they have no authority to nullify any of my magic if they are coming at me with ignorance and assumptions. I plan on fighting."

"Well, well. Look who's back! About time, Squirt. You had me worried."

"I've been busy."

"I figured. What with you running off without saying a word and taking Pandora with you," sniffed Adriana.

"We've been busy then. You aren't going to believe this, but we went to see Doreen and Donald Murphy."

"Oh, that's awful," said Adriana feigning shock.

"Funny. No, they called me to the motel because they've been housing Heathcliff Fitzwillow...and guess what? He's an agent of the Order. Or was."

"That explains the name. None of the agents I've ever met in my brief time with them had real names. They are all Fitz-something. I must be slipping...I should have realized this when I heard the man's name. Interesting."

"Yes, I pointed the Murphys in the direction of the police

department, and Dorie and I did something else highly entertaining.

"Dare I ask?"

"We went back to the Forbidden Library," I said proudly.

"Did you now?" said Adriana with some mirth.

"Yes. And I... wait. Why did you say it that way?"

"Say it what way?"

"It? No... stop! Why did you chuckle a bit when I told you I went to the Forbidden Library?"

"I didn't chuckle."

"Granny! Knock it off. You smirked a little."

"Liliana, you can't have it both ways. Either I chuckled or I smirked. Make up your mind."

"Listen you evil imp... don't trifle with me right now! I am not in the mood. Why did your personality change a bit when you... forget it. You knew. How did you know where I went?"

Adriana sighed and dusted off her skirt even though it was spotless. "I surmised you may have decided it would benefit you to go back and grill the Black Grimoire...so I kind of made sure Jerry was otherwise occupied. I just got an earful from him about an unauthorized visit to the library. I assume, by my stellar deduction abilities, that it was you who entered illegally?"

"In a manner of speaking."

"And I also assume it was you who dressed down those three uptight grims?"

Yeah...what? Grims?" I asked in confusion.

"Grims are magical beings who walk on both sides of the veil. Filbert, Clarice, and Theodosia are all grims."

"Theo-who-sia?"

"Yes, well, she's particular about her name so don't poke fun at Theo."

When I had leisure time, I would delve into these grims, but right now, I had a battle to plan. I also needed to clear my mind of anything and everything to do with Lorcan Reid. I steadfastly refused to believe in anything nefarious and prayed Lorcan knew what he was doing...because I sure as heck didn't. But I trusted him. I knew his soul. And I knew, deep inside, past all the layers of worry and doubt, that he'd never hurt me, intentionally or otherwise. So, I had to set aside the Tiffany and Lorcan equation and focus on the Tiffany and Lily one. That witch was going down.

"I have news that I gleaned at the Forbidden Library, for yes, indeed, it was me and Dorie and even Edith Plank...and boy did we find out some things about Sweet Briar Witches!"

"Really? And what did you find out?"

I didn't tell Adriana. Instead, I showed her. Abner wasn't the only one poking around the garden. The minute I'd arrived home, I immediate went to the only sweet briar rose bush I knew of in town and proceeded to carefully remove some of the rose hips and a few thorns and placed them in a burlap wrap that I'd carefully tied closed. I opened it now and showed Adriana my unexpected and incredible discovery.

Opening the burlap, I showed Adriana the bits and pieces from the little shrub outside my door, but then proceeded to knock her socks off with an unexpected and amazing turn of events.

"Sweet Briar Witches can make formidable magic using the petals, rosehips, and thorns from a sweet briar rose. The thorns are especially potent...look."

Holding my hands out toward the thorns, Adriana watched as they began to turn into green vines, then burst open with big, pink rose blossoms.

"Whoa."

"Indeed."

"But you aren't to perform any magic, Liliana. The Council…"

"The Council won't know a thing because I'm not performing magic. The sweet briar rose is reacting to my presence. I command the bush. I am a Sweet Briar Witch." I said this with a flourish, then waved my hands and the blossoms and vines disappeared.

Adriana sat back in astonishment, blinking at me like a wise old owl, then grinned…erasing years from her face.

Holding her hands out in the same manner did not yield the same results. The thorns and rosehips remained as so.

"Ah, well. I thought I'd give it a try. This is new territory for me, kid. You are the first Sweet Briar Witch in… well, I don't know how long. And that's a long time."

"And I am not a bringer of destruction, despite what those premonitions say. I found more information buried deep in the Fuchsia Grimoire that…"

"You what? The Fuchsia Grimoire? But that book is the stuff of legend. There is no such thing!"

"Yet there is, and Tiffany Clarkson of the Sweet Briar Clarksons managed to open and read it…and steal the recipe for a dangerous and destructive poison. I believe she intends to make it look like I am the one who…well, I'm not sure what she has planned. However, I do know one thing. The Fuchsia Grimoire is the property of the Sweet Briar Witch. That is MY book, and once it recognized me, boy oh boy, did it start talking. Especially about blood and blood sacrifice."

"Wait. How did Tiffany open the book…how did she manage to get into the library in the first place?"

"Just what I said. Blood. Specifically, my blood. Somehow, Tiffany Clarkson managed to get a hold of some of my blood and used it to gain entry to the library and converse with the Fuchsia Grimoire, although, after a few moments, the book realized the treachery and shut down before Tiffany could get all of its secrets."

"Well, duh. Sheriff Glen had you tested for drugs at the jail when you were arrested. You gave two vials of blood. That must have been when...or how...Tiffany swiped a vial, or even both. That little minx!" Adriana was fuming, and so was I.

"I remember getting poked and prodded by Shirley Jones, but I didn't think anything of it. She was apologetic and Tiffany was nowhere in sight...especially after her little fake strip search joke. I was so frazzled; I didn't even remember giving blood!"

"Standard to get a drug test around here. Especially since witches can do some funky magic when mixing human narcotics. Tiffany, being a cop, knew what was coming and probably took both the vials. We need to figure out what she is planning."

Adriana looked down as her cell phone jangled. "It's Gloria Stillwell. I wonder what she wants?"

My great-grandmother answered the call, and I watched as a range of emotions crossed her face. I became slightly concerned when she glanced up at me then looked away before sighing slightly.

"I hear you, Gloria. And I thank you; you're a true friend. I will. She's right here. Yes...OK, see you tomorrow."

"Dare I ask how bad the news coming from Gloria is?" I asked when Adriana disconnected her cell.

"It's not as bad as you're probably thinking, but it's not great. Too many variables."

"Oh?"

"It seems Gloria has been on the phone with Maybelle all morning, and she is frantic with worry about her precious daughter."

"Who is Maybelle, and why does this concern me?"

"Maybelle is Maybelle Abernathy Clarkson of the Sweet Briar Clarksons. Tiffany's mother."

"Oh, great. What's up her..."

"Liliana."

I sighed and clamped my mouth shut.

"Maybelle isn't all that bad. I believe she is being influenced by Wilhelmina and a few other hostile families against us, and if it weren't for her tightwad snot of a husband, Ebenezer, she'd probably be on our side."

"Ebenezer? Maybelle? Wilhelmina. Who gives their children names like that?" I asked.

"Who names them Tiffany? I mean really," sniffed Adriana.

"Tiffany is quite common, I think."

"It's a crime against nature."

"You had an ancestor named Lucretia; you should talk," I cried.

"She's you ancestor as well."

True. That.

"Witches, especially of a certain age, tend to like extreme names, but Tiffany is just wrong."

"In so many ways, as far as this one goes. So, what gives?"

"She found Lucifer dead in her yard."

OK. If there was one thing I expected to come out of my great-grandmother's mouth, that wasn't it.

"How did she know she was looking at Lucifer? I mean, how could Maybelle Clarkson know what the Devil looked like, anyway?"

"Not *the* Devil, you imbecile, the rabbit. Tiffany's rabbit!"

"Oh." *And hey!*

"Yes, oh. And what's more, it looks like he's been...well. It looks like someone did away with him and drained his blood."

Ew. I might not like Tiffany or her lousy rabbit, taking all of Lorcan's time doing stupid rabbit escape maneuvers, making Lor have to go rescue him, but I didn't like that someone killed the poor thing!

Then I began to connect the dots.

"Oh my gosh! Tiffany. She killed her own rabbit for a blood sacrifice. Just what the Fuchsia Grimoire warned me of. Tiffany is going to try some kind of murder that will harm everyone at the Council...and blame it on me."

"Tiffany isn't going to be able to fool anyone at this point. Maybelle already spoke with Sheriff Buford. Glen is trying to find Tiffany even as we speak, but she isn't answering her phone or..."

"Lorcan! He's with her. I need to go find him!"

"Why is Lorcan with Tiffany?" asked Adriana.

"Abner said she hired him to be an agent with another person and they are guarding the Council tonight. I need to get word to him. Granny, he's in danger."

No, he isn't. Trust the process. Trust Lorcan.

"Yes, he is. He..." belatedly, I realized it was Wicked who spoke, and I stopped arguing my point.

"I didn't say he wasn't. Why are you arguing with me?"

I looked from Adriana to Wicked and back, then realized my great-grandmother hadn't heard anything and stopped myself from explaining.

"I'm tired. I need to rest so I'm ready for tomorrow. What is going to happen now?"

"Now I think I need to get word to this Delvin character and your cousin Maggie, protocol be damned. They need to know we are dealing with a real rogue witch, and it certainly isn't you."

"But the inquest, my trail of sorts..."

"Will still go on. We need a plan, and I don't have time to waste on you when I need to contact the head of the Order!"

I sat back, shocked at Adriana's harsh words. She realized how it must have sounded to me because she shook her head and reached her hands out, gripping mine, and began to explain.

"Liliana. You are a strong witch. You don't need me to coddle you. Unfortunately, if Tiffany has gone off her rocker and is plotting something terrible, I need to reach Delvin Fitzwick. Tiffany already murdered an agent of the Order...since we know she took out Heathcliff. Delvin must know this, and I need to coordinate with Glen. I need to meet with Gloria, and we have to plot a strategy for tomorrow."

"But I should..."

"You should nothing!" Adriana raised her voice and frowned at me.

"Liliana...my dear. You need to get your rest—you are correct about needing plenty of it. And you need to be kept in the dark." I went to protest, but Adriana held up her hand stopping me. "If we are to trap Tiffany and you are to be her mark, you need to be shocked and off-balance when she confronts you tomorrow—and confront you she will. If you are prepared, Tiffany will see right through it. She might be a lunatic, but she is one who has been trained by not only the police, but the military. You have to be kept in the dark."

"But that means I will fight blind when it comes time to fight."

"And I know of no one better in a dark magic battle than you, my dear."

Adriana's vote of confidence had me tearing up. I knew, by this point, when I called up my dark magic it never failed me, and I was a formidable dark witch, but hearing her say it had me choked up with emotions.

"Now, now, enough of that nonsense. Go to sleep, Liliana. Tomorrow, all you need to do is show up and be prepared for anything—and trust your family and friends. We won't let you down."

"Meow!" Wicked added her two cents, causing Adriana to laugh as well as breaking the tension. I reached down to scratch her behind the ears, earning a loud purr for my efforts.

"OK, I will turn in for the night. But Wicked is coming with me tomorrow. And no one better try and stop her from entering the chamber."

"I'd like to see them try," said Adriana.

So would I.

17

Talk about walking in blind. I arrived at the Witch Council alone, Wicked my only companion. No one gave Wicked a second glance—I guess everyone was used to her as my shadow. I was escorted to the chamber and thankfully found Jake Carter waiting for me at the door. He'd called after Adriana departed last night and we went over strategy, and I informed him of everything I knew and everything Adriana told me.

Jake informed me he'd put in a few calls to Judge Cornelius and Delvin Fitzwick himself, but that didn't stop the trial and insanity of accusations coming from our enemies.

"It has come to our attention that as this Sweet Briar Witch, you have the power in hand to bring about the destruction of our world. In fact, we have it under the highest authority that your goal is to destroy this Witch Council, all of the Elders present today, and start your own authority anew once you've removed any and all who would stand in your way," stated Delvin, glaring at me like I was about to morph into a demon and rain brimstone and fire down upon the committee. The accusations had been going on for the better part of two hours, and I was becoming groggy with boredom. Everything being thrown at me was hearsay, and even I knew it.

"As I've stated before, your so-called 'highest authority' is slander coming from the Dietrich, Langsford, Plank, Clarkson, Witherspoon, Harding, Warren, Bolger, Espinosa, Nightingale, Peroni, Kowalski, Brentwood and Goldstein families along with some minor witch folk and townsfolk who have decided to form a gang of malcontent and try to usurp the Dolce authority," stated Jake, looking rather bored.

All those families hated mine. It made no sense. In the short time I've been in Sweet Briar, I've never once done anything to harm these people. Much. I mean Edith Plank is dead...but my friend now. I could understand the Nightingale family...but it's not my fault Rowan is a tilty-head freak show on the run from the law. I did almost burn down the town, but my great-grandfather Antonio cleaned it up. OK, so he turned old Doc Warren into a sheep. Hmm, on further thought, we might be slightly menacing to some. But still! Most of those names I didn't even recognize.

There was no sign of Tiffany—or Lorcan for that matter, which had me concerned. Gloria arrived at the Council with four of the Elders last night and found everything quiet. A cursory drive by Lorcan's place showed darkened windows— Eileen and Henry had no idea where he was. I felt mildly ill when I realized he was probably out with Tiffany all night. But I believed in him still—nothing would stop that. I prayed that he didn't come to harm, and my worry had no bounds. I hoped whatever plans my friends and family made were in place and they expected the unexpected.

Breathe, Lily. We have your back.

Blinking, I glanced down at Wicked and smiled. She wasn't paying any attention to me but remained transfixed on one of the darkened archways that concealed some of my audience. One thing I hated about this chamber was the lack of lighting and ability to see who was watching you from the eaves. It was disconcerting to say the least. Wicked, however, seemed to be able to see perfectly fine, and when she began to growl, the hairs on my arms stood on end.

Cousin Nora stepped out from under the arch and made eye contact with me. I could just make out someone behind her and thought it might be Tiffany.

Belatedly, I considered Nora might be the third person Tiffany hired to be an agent, and all the doubt of her true intensions came flooding back, but then she gave me a tiny wink and a slight smile before the veil of boredom covered her face once more, and she sneered at me. If she was acting, it was a convincing performance, especially when she slowly made her way over to Stella Langsford and took a seat beside her, patting her hand for support. The shadowy figure remained hidden, but I knew it was Tiffany—Wicked hadn't stopped staring—or growling.

"What do you say to these claims?" Delvin demanded of me.

"Um..." Great time to have my mind wander. I didn't hear the charges before the question.

"Listen. I'd like to say something in my defense."

Delvin Fitzwick glanced at my cousin Maggie who nodded, and I felt myself relax.

"Proceed."

Clearing my throat slightly, I began to speak.

"I came to Sweet Briar, as many of you know, not comprehending I was a witch. Or any Breed. I didn't even know what Breed meant. I had dark magic clouding me, damaging my family, ruining our memories, destroying us slowly. Over time and with the help of many, I was able to discover the evil behind these attacks and went after it. Unfortunately, there were some casualties along the way, but even though I am a dark witch, I am not an evil person. I would never go out of my way to cause harm. Quite the opposite really, I just want to make my art, live my life, get married someday...be normal. Why on earth would I scheme and plot and cause havoc in the town I now call home?"

"Because you are evil. Evil. Look at me...look at what Lily Sweet did to me when she discovered her lover in my arms!" Tiffany Clarkson of the Sweet Briar Clarksons came rushing into the room, battered and bloody and fell to her knees in front of Delvin Fitzwick who jumped back.

"Who is this person?" he cried.

"Tiffany! That's my child!" cried a man from the front seats, who could only be Ebenezer Clarkson.

"That is my deputy," said Glen Buford. The sheriff, much to his credit, looked shocked and concerned on Tiffany's behalf, even as he and Gloria Stillwell came to stand beside her. He even knelt down and helped Tiffany to her feet. The mien of apprehension and care on Gloria's face had a trickle of doubt and fear course through me...perhaps? But no. Gloria is on my side. Right?

Steady, Lily. Steady.

Wicked's words eased my tension once more, and I unclenched my jaw which was aching at this point.

"What happened, Tiffany?" asked Gloria with concern.

"She killed my rabbit! She killed my baby bunny. Then she attacked me. Lorcan...well, we've been getting close. I didn't mean for it to happen, but you can't stop true love. We've been getting close, and he's been trying to figure out a way to break it off with Lily when she discovered us together. She went crazy! Lily attacked me with dark magic. Blood magic. I'm covered in her blood!"

"No! She would never," cried Eileen from the sidelines.

"How could Lily do magic when she is being traced? The Council would know the minute she did."

"She's a powerful dark witch. If you don't believe me, run a wand over my scratches...Lily's blood is mixed with mine!" wailed Tiffany, pitifully.

Gloria pulled her wand out and ran it up and down the length of Tiffany's bruised and battered body. Then her head shot up and she addressed the Elders. "This is Lily Sweet's blood."

The room exploded with voices shouting out accusations and questions...along with those in support of me, but they seemed to be diminished slightly.

"There's more!" shouted Tiffany, now emboldened by the support she was getting from the audience of witches. "If you look around the room, you will find tiny gas globes filled with a noxious pink something or other. Lily did this. I saw her sneak in here early yesterday evening when I made my second patrol. I think she intends to harm everyone in this room. Please...please be careful. Guard yourself lest she make a move. Bind her. Now. Nullify her magic before it's too late."

Tiffany made to lunge at me, but Gloria stopped her, pinning her arms behind her back. It appeared she was whispering soothing words to calm Tiffany, but I wasn't certain what was going on.

"If I may?"

A voice from my left gave my spirits the boost it needed as Adriana Dolce stepped into the light.

"Good evening. It seems we are once again gathered in the chamber built with Dolce funds, in a building built with Dolce funds, in a town resurrected from a sleepy backwoods village to a tourist destination par excellence, a thriving and happy place with a booming economy all due to Dolce funds. Yet, it seems there is a never-ending wave of dissatisfaction from those who have never once lifted a finger to better this town, yet now want to reap the benefits of what was sown."

Adriana folded her hands in front of her.

"You aligned yourselves with an imbecile, however, if you remotely believe a word coming out of Tiffany's mouth."

"How dare you, vile witch. No one will listen to you any longer, Adriana. Not when it was you who helped your great-granddaughter with this foul magic. How else could Lily have discovered how to use such dark arcane knowledge?" shrieked Tiffany.

Before anyone could respond—especially Adriana, Tiffany wrenched her hand away from Gloria's hold and tossed a hefty spell in my great-grandmother's direction. Instead of deflecting it, the spell slammed into Adriana who stiffened, then slumped slightly.

"No!" I screamed.

Calling up my magic happened so fast, not one witch present could even think I'd do just that before I had my dark witch power on full alert with my siren magic swirling as backup. I crackled and dazzled with streams of power coursing around me.

"See? Look at how dangerous Lily is. They care nothing for you. They stick together and would harm everyone present for their gain."

"You noxious little twit. Leave my daughter alone." Adelaide appeared behind me as did Charlie, their own magic on full display. The air smelled of sulphur and fury—it was vibrating with danger, yet I remained calm and focused. My black eyes never leaving those of Tiffany's, who I could now clearly see, were bold with madness. How no one else could see the blatant look of mental disarray was beyond me. Tiffany was frothing and giggling in irrational glee, assured of her victory.

"Look! Even now the globes are absorbing Lily's magic.

She is preparing to smite all of us!" screamed Tiffany as she threw her head back and stretched her arms wide. Gloria reached out and pinned Tiffany's arms back once more.

All eyes turned upward as traces of my magic did indeed appear to be winding and coiling their way in the air where they were sucked into the gas globes which slightly expanded. So that's how Tiffany would prove I was behind this. The spell she learned was of mass destruction, and my stolen blood along with the magic behind it recognized the spell from the Fuchsia Grimoire. It was diabolical...and I had to give Tiffany credit. It might work.

No one can stop the Sweet Briar Witch. Lily Sweet is the one you have feared all this time, but your fear is misplaced. The Sweet Briar Witch brings change, yes, but she is the catalyst for change—for the good of all. All she touches grows fruitful and benefits even as the sweet briar rose thrives and expands. Even now, her magic is protecting us all.

Amazingly to me and everyone present, Wicked's voice reached all ears, yet no one seemed to know who it was that had spoken. Heads were turning this way and that trying to discover the speaker to no avail. No one thought to look down at a furry black kitty sitting smug and perfect in the center of the room.

While I was busy smiling down at Wicked, I had noticed the gasps coming from those gathered until I happened to glance down at myself. Vines were growing out of me with thorns and blossoms sprouting forth. I was turning into a giant sweet briar rose bush!

"Stop this nonsense. All of you. I would never harm anyone in this room unless they tried to harm me or those I love. I am the Sweet Briar Witch, but I didn't make those gas globes. Tiffany did."

"Liar!"

"Am I? Did you not break into the Forbidden Library and

force Clarice to do your bidding, attempting to learn the secrets from the Fuchsia Grimoire before it slammed shut at your deception? Did you not put a spell on Lorcan and bug his shop so you could discover information to use to have me think he doesn't love me anymore? And did you not meet with then murder, Heathcliff Fitzwillow by summoning demons on the Dietrich estate then try to blame me for it?"

"You lie, Lily Sweet. Lorcan came to me. Beseeching me for help! He told me you ordered him to attack the Elders and the representatives from the Order should they vote against you. He begged me for help."

"You are delusional, Tiffany. And you need professional help getting that head of yours cleared of such nonsense."

I turned away from crazy and approached the dais. Upon reaching Delvin and Maggie, I called in my magic, erasing the vines and flowers, yet held the thorns in my hand. I dialed down my dark witch magic and allowed the siren magic to dissipate lest anyone think I'd use it to enchant. Basically, I left myself open to attack, yet prepared to counter—and no one here could fault me for that.

Opening my hands, I showed the sweet briar rose thorns to Delvin. "I command the magic of the Sweet Briar Witch. With my power I can easily smite this town, all present and go on a rampage. So how come I haven't yet? Because I am not a madwoman frothing at the mouth with her misconceptions. There is only one person present who is doing so at the moment." Cutting my eyes to Tiffany then returning them to Delvin, I continued, "And it certainly isn't me."

Delvin gave me an imploring look and glanced up at the globes as if to say, "What do we do about those?" But instead, he turned to address the room.

"This witch is dangerous. Even now those globes are expanding and will burst in time, taking us all out with the foulest of magic."

Another gasp went through the crowd as Delvin continued.

"As it is decreed that only one bound to you can stop you. We have to trust in Lorcan Reid to do the right thing and not only nullify your magic but stop you with force—and more—should you make a move to destroy everyone present. We discovered this when researching the other Sweet Briar Witch known to be in existence, your cousin Tarni Vanderzee. Only one bound to one such as you can nullify your dark magic and stop you. Are we to understand you have commanded your lover to not make a move against us should we vote not be in your favor?"

"Lorcan would never harm me. We are a team," I replied softly.

"Liar!" screeched Tiffany. Everything you spew is lies, Lily Sweet."

Tiffany broke away from the hold Gloria Stillwell had on her and approached the dais.

"Unlike Tarni and her lover, Logan, Lorcan Reid would never allow you to live if he knew it meant the end of Sweet Briar and all the Breed who called this place home!" cried Tiffany, looking every bit the lunatic. "He would never let harm come to the innocent. And if he were here, he'd stop you. What have you done to poor Lorcan? We need him present to destroy your maniacal hold on us all! He would never let your magic harm us!"

"That was your mistake right there, Tiffany." Lorcan stepped out from behind the column near the podium, shocking everyone with his sudden bedraggled appearance. He looked worse than Tiffany, and I almost broke my calm demeanor when I saw how bloodied and battered he was.

"You assumed I'd remain a mild-mannered and gentle man when it came down to it. Not cause waves. Not put anyone or anything in harm's way and allow bad things to happen to Lily.

You miscalculated, and your assumptions will be your downfall. I, too, will let the world burn to save the woman I love," said Lorcan. Then he dove toward the podium, hitting a hidden switch, allowing the toxic magic to explode from the globes and pour into the Witch Council, much to the astonishment of all.

I felt my heart swelling even as I considered what this might mean to everyone present.

I didn't waste another second of time and let loose the last bit of my dark magic held on reserve which flew across the room and directly into the maniacal witch who dropped like a stone. Tiffany was down for the count.

And just like that, the threat to everyone I loved and a few I loathed was over.

"Now, Pandora!" Lorcan called out to the crossroads demon who launched herself into the center of the room and sent out her own brand of wicked magic which oozed from her hands—all black smoke and inky darkness—and absorbed every last bit of the toxic fumes that were circulating the chamber.

Overwhelming relief slammed into me, and while I secretly appreciated the fact Lorcan would have sacrificed everyone present, I was equally thrilled he and Dorie cooked up a plan unbeknownst to any of us... and I would never hold it against them. We were otherwise occupied with yet another insane witch, after all—holding grudges was ridiculous.

"Lorcan!" I cried even as the man I loved rushed to my open arms.

"I'm here, Lily. And boy do I have a tale for you."

As chaos exploded around us with people rushing hither and yon and fires being put out, Lorcan Reid and I embraced, and I knew everything would be fine in my world.

18

"Is she going to be OK?" I asked the cleric who was looking over Adriana.

"She took quite a hit of magic that was tainted with insanity, but she should pull through just fine. Adriana is a tough old bird," whispered the cleric.

"I wouldn't say that much louder. Adriana is crafty and can probably hear everything we're saying," said Lorcan with a smile for the woman.

The cleric blanched, glancing down at Adriana, and I chuckled. "I'm sure you are fine. She won't be turning anyone into weeds any time soon."

I saw a slight smile appear on my great-grandmother's face and knew everything would be OK, and I sighed in relief even though her eyes remained shut.

Leaving the cleric to continue caring for Adriana with Grandpa Antonio by her side, I followed Lorcan out to the waiting room and took a seat by the windows looking out at a lovely garden. Well, it would be in springtime...right now all it had to offer was a plethora of bird feeders with the tiny critters flitting back and forth grabbing seeds.

In the waiting room was a crowd of people all here in support of Adriana, my family, and...in some ways, me.

Of course, I was cleared of any wrongdoing, much to the dismay of our enemies. But even Ebenezer Clarkson of the Sweet Briar Clarksons had to back down when his wife, Maybelle, came forward with what she'd discovered regarding Tiffany.

As for old Tiff, she was locked away in the loony bin at the witch hospital and undergoing mental evaluations. I heard she'd failed most if not all of them so far.

The Elders for and against me voted, and they not only cleared me of all accusations, but they also decreed that while my basic magic was wonky and needed work, I didn't appear to be a threat, should get my Elder status back...and could marry whomever the heck I felt like marrying.

Which was one reason I didn't like the way Lorcan kept glancing at me then away like he had the weight of the world on his shoulders.

I decided right then to get to the bottom of everything and motioned to everyone present I needed a minute. Pandora nodded and began recounting her end of the story, entertaining everyone with her acts of daredevil. Pulling Lorcan out of the room and down a small corridor, I placed my hands on either side of his face.

"What is it? You look like the most miserable man out there. Didn't the clerics make all the pain go away? Your face looks great...are you still hurting?"

"My body might be fine but my heart hurts."

I placed my head to Lorcan's chest and listened. Worried he might be ill, I made to pull him back toward the ER and a doctor, but he stopped me.

"Not like that, Lily. Listen..." Sighing, Lorcan pulled me over to a bench and sat me down. "I had to pretend I was attracted to Tiffany. I suspected she was up to something for some time now and also thought she might have bugged my shop in some way...although I've never been able to find anything. Of course, I had to be careful in my search so as not to tip her I suspected anything. Now? I plan on tearing my place apart until I find something."

I smiled and stroked his face. He seemed so worried. I felt butterflies in my stomach knowing I wasn't going to like what he had to say.

"In my attempt to fool Tiffany, I may have kissed her a time or two. Nothing too intense—but last night I had to lay it on thick. However, she suspected something was up and attacked me. She waited for me to start patrolling the Council then pounced. I didn't see or hear a thing coming but Tiffany stupidly forgot to bind me, and I wandered out and texted Pandora right away, knowing I needed to reach out to someone. Stu gave me his spare phone in case Tiffany took mine, and I'm glad he did. That was the first thing Tiffany destroyed...but with Stu's tucked in my boot, I had backup. It's just...Lily. I'm sorry I kissed Tiffany. Can you forgive me? I couldn't approach you with this knowing we might lose the chance at nabbing that crazy witch!"

"Did you like kissing her?"

"What do you think?"

"I think I'd rather not think about you kissing Tiffany."

Lorcan hung his head, and I couldn't let him continue to berate himself. While I didn't like what he did, I knew he had to handle things his way, and it might have jeopardized ever revealing Tiffany's treachery if he pushed her away. Let's face it...she'd still be a police officer and she'd still be waiting for me to slip up or who knows what. Now? Now Tiffany is cooling her heels in the mental ward, and I hoped it would be the last we'd ever see of the witch. Well, except for her upcoming trial in a few months. I'm sure that will be loads of fun.

Not.

"We're good, Lor...better than good. We're free of that shrew."

"I'm just sorry I didn't believe you at first. But you were right."

"Come again?"

Lorcan smiled and gave me a half hug. "You heard me. I said you were right."

"Well, I certainly won't get tired of hearing those words come out of your mouth."

Just then Nora walked by, and I stopped her much to her surprise.

"Thank you. For your help in this."

"But I didn't do much," protested Nora, looking back and forth between Lorcan and me.

"If you hadn't given me that little wink this morning, I might have let my nerves and doubts get the better of me. Nora, that bolstered my confidence that I could trust my friends...and family. You might not think it much, but I thank you."

Nora ducked her head and nodded, then whispered something I couldn't make out, moving to join our family. That was a fence that needed mending a tad longer before all was right again. I let her go and turned to Lorcan once more.

"Maggie remained behind after Delvin Fitzwick departed. I'm glad he listened to Gloria and Sheriff Glen as well. That was an insane story your family brought to them. Summoning demons and creating gas globes. Tiffany never stood a chance though...she was too insane to plot anything that made sense...and certainly didn't do anything methodically. Now you, my dear, if you set your mind to nefarious destruction? We'd all be in trouble."

"Aw...Lor, that is the sweetest thing you've ever said to me."

"So, we're good?" he asked once more.

"We're good. But I may wash your mouth out with soap, rinse, and repeat?"

"Have your way with me, woman."

Pandora came rushing into the corridor, followed by Wicked.

"Hey, guys. Do you think we'll ever get this mess straightened out? I have so many questions," she asked.

"You and me both, Dorie. But let's just say Tiffany has been at this craziness for a while now and had the ear of poor Heathcliff Fitzwillow for a long time before he grew suspicious and came to see what was what on his own. Had she just been content to sow the seeds of doubt and leave it at that, she might have gotten more traction with those lies about me. But once Heathcliff showed up here in Sweet Briar, she had to have known he suspected something was off. Then she did away with him...and all her crazy plans unraveled, only she is so delusional she went with it anyway," I said.

Of course, I'd like to know why I seemed to attract crazy witches and their evil visions of grandeur, but I'd leave that for another day. I was too busy watching a nervous Pandora fret and wring her hands, while glancing over her shoulder repeatedly.

"What's with you?" I asked her.

"Oh nothing I... eek!"

Running away from us and toward an exit door, my answer came in the form of my cousin Maggie, as she charged after the crossroads demon.

"Oh no you don't. Pandora! Get over here. Care to explain what you and Ellie got up to in Texas and why New Orleans is overrun with rampaging pixies? Pandora! You better explain yourself! Get back here!"

And they were off while Lorcan and I remained behind

laughing at the sight. I glanced down when Wicked began to wind her way around my ankles.

"What about you? Care to inform me why and how you are now speaking in my mind? And how you managed to do what you did at the Witch Council?"

"What are you talking about, Lily?" asked Lorcan.

"Wicked has been speaking—in English—in my head. She...what? Stop looking at me like that!"

Lorcan gazed at Wicked then locked his eyes to mine.

"Lily...cats can't speak."

"Oh no? Wicked, here has been doing just that. For weeks now!"

We both looked down at Wicked who began washing her fur, indifferent and aloof.

"Wicked tell him. Tell Lorcan. Say something and prove that you've been speaking to me."

"Merowoo?"

"Oh, knock it off, Wicked! You know that you've been speaking to me. Don't try to make me look like a loon. Now, speak."

Standing up and stretching languidly then blinking a few times, Wicked proceeded to turn around, flop over and wash her nether regions.

"Um, Lily?"

"Don't you dare, Lorcan Reid. I am telling you right now. I will get that cat to prove to everyone I know that she's been speaking to me or die trying. You'll see. Wicked will speak!"

Care to make a bet?

Thank you for reading! I hope you loved meeting Lily and Lorcan, and the rest of the characters. The next book in the

Lily Sweet Mysteries is Spells Like A Witch coming Summer 2022.

And if you enjoyed I Spell Trouble, you'll love Lily's cousin Maggie, and her quirky, sometimes funny, sometimes dark, but always magical paranormal gang of monster-hunting antique appraisers. A Tale of Two Sisters, the tie-in series to my Lily Sweet World, highlights Lily's cousins Maggie and Ellie Fortune and is FREE on Kindle Unlimited!

"I am loving the snark in this book."

- S. Keller, BookBub author reviews.

And if two series wasn't enough, I'd like to introduce you to siren, Tarni Vanderzee in the first in the Secret Siren series: SIREN RISE. Refusing conformity. Embracing the unknown. Accepting what life throws her way over an oppressive past can bring Tarni ultimate joy...or total ruin!

I appreciate your help in spreading the word, including telling friends and family. Reviews help readers find books! Please leave a review on your favorite book site.

You can also join my Facebook Group: Author Bettina M. Johnson's Team Wicked for exclusive giveaways and sneak peek of future books—and just plain silliness!

SIGN UP FOR BETTINA M. JOHNSON'S NEWSLETTER: http://eepurl.com/gZKo51

SOCIAL MEDIA LINKS

I write in my own style that may not be everyone's cup of tea —so if you enjoy my characters and humor, my plots, how the storyline is developing, etc. and are eagerly anticipating the next in the series, be aware that I am just as excited as you are—I've found someone who thinks my story ideas are neat! That is thrilling for any writer to know (or it should be). THANK YOU!

Visit my official website to receive updates, find out about special offers and new releases, or read my blog about writing and farm life - complete with photos - you might even catch me mowing my ten acres (seriously): http://www. bettinamjohnson.net

For more information or to contact me:
author@bettinamjohnson.net

For even more (if you just can't enough of me) follow my
Social Media Links

Mailing List - https://bit.ly/2BvQXmP
BookBub - https://bit.ly/2Epejwj
Goodreads - https://bit.ly/3aTejQW
Author Page - Amazon - https://amzn.to/3lj7L2L
Instagram - https://bit.ly/2QpZao1
TikTok - https://bit.ly/2PQa6Hg
MeWe - https://bit.ly/36A2RcM
Facebook - https://bit.ly/3gOaFZY
Twitter: https://bit.ly/3jahMgY
YouTube - https://bit.ly/2Stvy2X

ABOUT THE AUTHOR

I always knew I wanted to write. As a kid, way before the technology age had hit, I'd be stuck in the car with the folks as we drove from our home on Staten Island, NY, where I was born and raised, to our family property in the Catskill Mountains. To drive away boredom, I would sit, staring out the window, and create adventures of daring thieves riding horseback along the road, trying to escape the law. Other times I'd imagine a wild girl riding her unicorn into battle (I had a vivid imagination - we didn't have video games yet!).

As the years passed, I'd start writing a book, then stop, then start again only to let life get in the way, until one day I had an epiphany—a kick in the pants moment. If I waited any longer, all those wonderful characters in my head would never have their stories told, and that made me sad. So, I treated writing as my career. Once I started, it became apparent nothing would ever stop me again. YOU, dear reader, are stuck with me until I go off to that great library in the sky...or wherever writers go when they crumble to dust in front of their typewriters (or laptops...whatever!).

I live in the North Georgia mountains on what I like to call a farm, with my husband and almost adult kids, a Cairn Terrier, a bunch of cats, and fish. Occasionally other critters show up to keep things exciting.

BOOKS BY BETTINA M. JOHNSON

The Lily Sweet Mysteries:

Home Sweet Witch

Witch Way is Up?

How To Train Your Witch

Sweet Home Liliana

Witch Way Did He Go?

Revenge is Sweet, Witch

Witch and Peace

The Sweet Spell of Success

I Spell Trouble

Sweet Briar Witch

Spells Like a Witch (Coming Soon)

The Fortune-Telling Twins Mysteries:

A Tale of Two Sisters

Double Toil and Trouble

Fire and Earth, Sisters at Birth

Kindred Spirits

A Djinn and Tonic

A Werewolf in Sheep's Clothing

A Pocketful of Pixies (Coming Soon)

Secret Sirens

Siren Rise

Siren Star (March 2022)